IF WE FLY

A WHAT IF NOVEL

NINA LANE

SNOW QUEEN
PUBLISHING

If We Fly
A What If Novel

Published by Snow Queen Publishing

Cover photography: Sara Eirew
Cover design: Concierge Literary Designs & Photography

ISBN: 978-1-7360527-2-3

MJ Fryer and Maria D., this one is for you.
Thank you both so much.

PROLOGUE

Josie

Ten years ago

"How could you do that without telling me?" I zipped my art portfolio shut with a sharp movement and set it beside the door. "I have my art show prep the week before."

"Why didn't you put it on the calendar?" Cole turned from his computer, his thick-lashed blue eyes flashing with irritation. He shoved a spoon back into an open jar of peanut-butter and dark chocolate spread. "That's why we have a synced calendar, so we know what's going on."

"Your synced calendar is a pain to update. You can't even see an entire month at a time. That's why I bought the *wall calendar*." I flung my hand toward the Kandinsky calendar pinned up in our tiny kitchen. "You don't have to turn anything on to see what we have planned."

"So why isn't your art show prep on the *wall calendar* either?"

"It is! I wrote it down as soon as it was scheduled."

He jutted his chin to the calendar in a clear challenge. I stalked to the kitchen and flipped to the month of June, where almost every square contained an item written in Cole's block penmanship—Coastal Ecosystems, 12:00pm; work 4:00am; Aquarium, 2-4; Chemistry, 9:00am. All in black ink, the color he'd designated for himself. There was only one thing written in blue ink, which he'd informed me was my color.

"Look." I jabbed my finger at Friday, June twentieth. "Mom and Dad's twenty-fifth surprise anniversary party. Six o'clock, the Seagull Inn."

"And your *art show?*"

"I swear I wrote it down." I dropped the calendar pages in frustration. Multicolored Post-Its and taped notes decorating the front and side of the fridge caught my attention. I tore off a yellow note from beside the water dispenser and held it up triumphantly. "Here! Week of June fourth, art show prep."

"That is a refrigerator," Cole said in his deep, measured tone. "Not a calendar."

We glared at each other like wolves stalking their territory. Though the sight of my guy usually turned me all soft and mushy inside, I steeled myself against his potent effect. Tall and broad-shouldered with his faded Ford's College T-shirt stretched over his muscular chest, his sun-streaked brown hair rumpled, and his skin bronzed...he made me want to rub up against him like a cat stretching in the sun.

Except, at the moment, I was mad at him.

He narrowed his eyes. "Josephine."

"Colton." My irritation hardened again at his patronizing tone. "You know, for a man who lives by a freaking plan, I'm surprised you haven't started scheduling our sex life on the calendar."

"Who says I haven't?" He dug the spoon into the Choco-Nut and licked it, his eyebrow lifted.

"You lie like a rug. What about when we did it in the shower last week? You can't tell me you had that all planned out."

"Okay, I won't tell you that. And you're changing the subject."

"The *subject* is that you agreed to a camping trip with Lucy and Mike right before my art show." I grabbed a frozen pizza from the freezer and stabbed the oven preheat buttons. "At least you didn't rent the trailer."

His gaze suddenly shifted. He turned back to his computer.

I tossed the pizza on the counter in disbelief. "You did *not* already rent the trailer."

"There was a special deal," he replied defensively. "I didn't want to miss it."

"Oh my God." I threw my hands into the air. "You're like King Magus. He wouldn't even accept Zane's alliance offer before going after Lazarus because it hadn't been part of his *plan*. Then Lazarus launched that sneak attack and killed him, which I swear Zane would have—"

"Wait a minute." Cole rotated slowly in his swivel chair to face me. "Did you just say Lazarus kills Magus?"

Oh, shit.

"Uh...I mean, I might have read something—"

"You watched ahead, didn't you?" He rose to his feet and started toward me. Faint menace glinted in his eyes. "How many episodes?"

"Just...a few. Three, maybe." I backed up, my heart kicking up in gear. "Or four. Five! Five episodes, okay? I'm sorry. It's just that you get home so late, and I need to wind down a little before going to sleep so..."

He stopped in front of me, his arms crossed over his broad chest. God, he smelled good—like oranges, peanut butter, and dark chocolate. I stiffened my spine.

"Now you're changing the subject," I said.

"You were trying to get me thinking about sex." His expression darkened. "I am pointing out your transgression in watching *Empire of Gods* without me."

"What about *your* transgression in making plans without me?"

"I wouldn't have done that if you'd kept your part of the calendar updated."

"You totally would have. You have a very bad habit of making plans and scheduling stuff without asking me first."

"*You* have a very bad habit of not telling me what the hell you have going on."

"Well, with all our bad habits, maybe we shouldn't have moved in together in the first place!"

"Yeah, maybe not," he snapped.

I glowered. He glared. Tension sparked in the air.

"We should kiss," he finally said.

"Okay."

He stepped closer, backing me up against the wall and putting his hands on either side of my head. My anger slipped away, replaced by a combination of relief and the heady anticipation of a kiss from Cole Danforth. Even with space between us, *heat* radiated from his skin, like he'd absorbed the sun. Everything about him was always so warm, from his taut skin to the flare in his blue eyes.

He skimmed his gaze across my lips and lowered his mouth to mine. Arousal burst inside me. I loved the way he kissed me, as if he wanted to devour me. He held the sides of my neck and tilted my head to just the right angle before slipping his tongue past my lips. I curled my fingers into his shirt, my blood simmering. A familiar tension began to lace his body.

"What were we arguing about?" he muttered.

"I can't remember. Something about King Magus…"

"Doesn't matter anymore." He deepened the kiss and pressed me against the wall.

He cupped my breasts, rubbing my nipples through my shirt and bra. Shivers coursed through me, centering in my lower body. Slowly he pulled my shirt over my head and made quick work of my purple bra.

"So fucking perfect." He bent to kiss my breasts.

Heat swept through my veins. I gasped, driving my fingers into his thick hair, and pressed my thighs together. He could fire me up to a thousand in no time at all, and I *loved* it. He slipped his hand down into the waistband of my yoga pants. The instant he eased his long fingers into me, desire burst through me like an exploding star.

"Firecracker," he murmured. "Want me to set you off?"

A laugh rose to my throat. "Like the Fourth of July."

With a grin, he bent to tug my pants and cherry-printed panties off my legs, pressing a line of kisses down to my belly-button and back up to my breasts. He rose to his feet and leaned his forehead against mine, delving his fingers between my legs again.

I dragged in a breath. *God*, his touch was so expert, his fingers stroking all the right places. I pressed my face into his shoulder, straining toward the whirlwind of pleasure moving ever closer. Muffling my cry against his shoulder, I came sharp and fast.

Even as the vibrations still quivered through me, I urged us both into the bedroom. I tumbled back onto the bed, panting and aching for more.

With a snap of my fingers, I indicated his clothes. "Off."

He winked and stripped, revealing his incredible body—smooth skin burnished golden-brown from the sun; hard, well-defined pecs and a washboard stomach whose ridges I loved tracing with both my fingers and my tongue.

He climbed on top of me and lowered his mouth to mine. His kiss scorched me, fired me with fresh heat. My body, my heart, my soul—everything opened for him, welcomed him inside.

He filled me with slow, agonizingly delicious ease, his body a heavy weight between my thighs. I wrapped my arms and legs around him as he pulled back and pushed forward. We both fell, spiraling downward into the rhythmic cadence that now came so naturally to us.

"So good." I wiggled my hips. "I have an idea."

"What kind of idea?"

"An idea for an art series." I groaned and arched into him. "Let's cover ourselves with body paint and have sex on a bunch of big canvases. Whatever we create will be the artwork. Okay?"

He grabbed my hips and turned me over, giving my rear a little spank. "I'm not letting you display your perfect tits to the public."

"The way we mess around, I doubt anything will be recognizable." I got onto my hands and knees, closing my eyes when he pushed my thighs apart and positioned himself. "Will you...*oh!*"

He thrust into me, hard and deep. My body jerked forward, and then I was lost in the maelstrom of his heavy plunges.

"Okay?" I gasped.

"Why do you always ask me this kind of thing when we're fucking?" he grunted.

"Because I figure I have a better chance of you saying yes."

"You're right."

"So?"

"Goddamn..." He shoved so deep inside me I cried out. "Good thing I love you so much."

"A very good thing...oh my *God*, Cole..."

"Almost there...almost...*fuck*."

He stilled, a heavy growl rumbling from his throat as he gave in to his release. I loved it when he got all incoherent with lust, knowing I was the reason why. He pulled out of me with another groan and flopped down to tug me into his arms.

After slipping his hand between my legs, he brought me expertly to another shattering orgasm before we both lay there, chests heaving and bodies damp with sweat.

"I'll cancel the camping trip," he said.

"If I can get help with my art show, I might be able to work it out." I stroked his abdomen. "And what do you say about the canvases? I'll call it Love Smudges."

A hoarse chuckle broke from him. "You're a nut."

"Will you do it?"

"I'll do anything for you." He kissed my forehead. "Even make a print of my ass."

I grinned. "I promise I won't use any glue."

"Maybe it should be the color *blue*." He arched an eyebrow at me.

"Um...and we could practice kung *fu*."

He narrowed his eyes. "We'll just have to make *do*."

"Do you have any *shampoo*?"

"No, but I want a *tattoo*."

I looked at him in surprise. "Really?"

He laughed, a booming chuckle that warmed me like hot cocoa.

"*Really* does not rhyme with *tattoo*." He tugged a lock of my hair, his eyes creasing with amusement. "You lose, Josie Bird."

"You are such a *nerd*."

"Oh, no. Game's over." He curled his hand around the back of my neck and drew me in for another kiss. "But I still think my ass would look good in blue."

"Colton Danforth, I love *you*."

CHAPTER 1

Josie

Present

A red-gold sunrise paints the horizon and splashes over the cove, but the Water's Edge pier is desolate. The shops and restaurants are all dark and closed. Pigeons peck at crushed wrappers and bits of food. The carnival rides are still, the game booths shuttered.

On the Ocean Carousel, all the sea creatures are frozen in their various positions. Unlike ten years ago, they are now rundown and worn with flaking paint and faded colors. The two-seater whale is still grinning, but her red lipstick is peeling and much of the paint has chipped off her body.

Pulling my army jacket more closely around me, I turn away from the carousel and walk back to the pier entrance. My takeout coffee has grown bitter and cold in the hour I've been walking through town and along the beach.

Beyond a cracked concrete wall at the side of the pier, the docks bustle with workers and fishermen. Lobster boats stream toward the open sea.

Did Cole ever work on a lobster boat again after that night? Or was the accident a guillotine slicing his past and present in half?

I return to Lantern Square and unlock the storage cabinet where I keep all the paints and supplies for the mural. Though many of the town's residents have stopped by over the past weeks to help me paint the outlined scene, for safety reasons the festival committee barred anyone but me from using the mechanical lift they brought in to replace the scaffolding.

So I'm the only one who can paint the upper half of the mural —treetops, sky, the top of Eagle Mountain, the rooftops, the sun.

I set a few cans of paint on the lift and lever it upward to the top of the mural. Though birds are dotted throughout the lower half—chickadees, pigeons, ducks, sandpipers, warblers—the sky and trees are where I've outlined birds in flight.

Geese in a V-formation. Chickadees flying in a loose line. Finches in a neat oval. Ravens in a small family group.

As I work, carefully shading in the birds' feather colors and markings, the square comes to life for another day. People arrive to fetch their morning coffee at one of the cafés, a bus drops off a group of office workers, and the parking spaces fill with cars.

"It's a *gaggle* of geese, right?" My sister's voice rises from below.

"Yes." Shading my eyes from the ascending sun, I look down at her. In a loose summer maternity dress with her hair up in a ponytail, Vanessa looks lovely and more relaxed than I've seen her since I came back to Castille. "What are you doing here?"

"I have an early doctor's appointment, so I stopped to get a decaf latte." She holds up a frothy cup of coffee. "You want me to get you something?"

"No, thanks. I have one already." After lowering the lift, I climb off and approach her. "Do you want me to go with you to the doctor?"

"No, it's just a checkup." She pats her belly, then gestures to the mural. "It's really looking amazing. I love that you put in so many birds. A *kit* of pigeons."

"A charm of finches. A wisdom of owls." I look up at the ravens skimming past Eagle Mountain. "An unkindness of ravens."

"That's not very nice." She chuckles. "Clearly someone had something against black birds."

"Ravens are associated with the dead and lost souls." I wipe my hands on a rag and pick up another paintbrush. "An omen of bad luck."

"Are you sure you want them in the mural, then?"

"I've always liked them." I recall the plush raven Cole won for me at a carnival game booth a lifetime ago. Whatever happened to it? "They're intelligent, and they have a strong social structure. They mate for life."

"Certain men could take a lesson from them." Vanessa's lips twitch and she takes a sip of her latte. "Hey, I wanted to find out when I can take you out to celebrate your birthday. I know it was yesterday, but I had an...uh, appointment."

"An *appointment?*" I eye her with interest. "With a certain handsome police officer?"

Two pink spots color her cheeks. "Nathan and I might have had dinner last night."

"Wow. From coffee to dinner in less than a week? I'm impressed."

She nudges me in the arm. "What about your end of the bargain? Did you make a friend?"

"I tried and failed." I twist my mouth, thinking of Charlotte the librarian who turned down my 'let's hang out' offer. "I'll try again."

"Please do. And if you're free tonight, do you want to go over to that new Mexican restaurant in Benton? I heard they have great daiquiris."

"Sure. Thanks."

"I'll text you." She nods toward the mural. "Really nice work. I might have to attend the unveiling ceremony after all."

She waves and starts toward the street corner.

"Vanessa."

She turns, her eyebrows lifted. Anxiety ripples down my spine.

"Do you remember a keychain Dad once had?" I tighten my grip on the paintbrush. "The letter B Teddy had made in woodshop."

Her forehead creases. "I think so. Why?"

"There's a picture of all of us at the inn right before the accident," I explain. "I was holding the keychain. I was just wondering what happened to it."

"I haven't seen it." A shadow passes over her features. "We got all the personal stuff back from the police or the impound lot. The keychain is probably in the same box."

"Where is all that?"

"Either it got thrown out, or it's in the basement." She shrugs. "I don't know. I didn't go through any of it. Why are you asking?"

"Just curious." I force out a breath. "Hey, do you mind if I borrow your car this afternoon?"

"Sure. I'll drop it off after my appointment and walk home. I need the exercise."

"Thanks. Call me when you're done and let me know how everything is going."

After she leaves, I continue painting the birds. I can't get the image of the photograph out of my mind, as if it's been burned there. Why do I not remember holding my father's big, unwieldy keychain? Why do I not remember giving the keys to Cole before we left the restaurant?

For ten years, posing for that photo and the snap of the

shutter has been my last memory of that night until I woke up in the hospital, wounded and shattered. I remember the smell of wildflowers, the weight of my mother's arm around me, the noise from the lingering guests.

Then it's like I leapt off a cliff into a black, empty void.

How do I not remember the fucking keychain?

My father carried it everywhere. It had all his keys—house, car, office, garage. When the car key was in the ignition, the wooden letter B would almost bump against his knee, and my father hadn't been very tall. Considering Cole's height and the fact that his legs are so long, it must have really annoyed him when he was driving the SUV.

A headache pushes between my eyes. I color a raven's body with pitch-black paint. Three "unkindnesses" of ravens fly across the mural, their wings spread. Unlike crows, who tend to flap their wings, ravens soar and glide through the sky.

"How's the weather up there, Josie Bird?" Cole's voice, warm and deep, slides into my blood.

"Same as it is down there." I set the paintbrush down and lower the lift, feeling his eyes on me as if he's touching me.

"You left early." He frowns, skimming his gaze to my lips. "And you didn't say goodbye."

"Couldn't sleep, so I figured I'd get some stuff done. I left you a note that I'd take the bus back to town." Rubbing my hands on my overalls, I drink him in—tailored navy suit and tie, perfectly starched white shirt, his hair gleaming golden-brown in the early sunlight. I want to close the distance between us, tuck my body against his, feel his strong arms close hard around me.

Clearing my throat, I step back, conscious of people passing by. "I'm going to go out with Vanessa tonight. She wants to treat me to dinner for my birthday."

"Okay. I'll be working late, so text if you need anything." He starts toward the side door of the Snapdragon Inn. "You got your coffee? House keys? Red Lifesavers and Jolly Ranchers? Lunch money?"

A smile nudges at my heart. "And my brand-new red backpack."

"Okay." He tilts his chin to his office window five stories up. "I'll be keeping an eye on you."

He winks at me and strides into the inn. I watch him go, appreciating his long legs and the breadth of his shoulders beneath his suit jacket.

Turning away slowly, I refocus on the mural. A morning crowd starts to gather, and several people ask to paint. At one, I hang out the "Back Soon" sign and walk to Dandelion Street, where Vanessa texted me that she parked her rattling old Dodge. I take out the spare key she'd given me, and I get into the driver's seat.

Gripping the wheel, I pull in a long breath. After the accident, I'd struggled to do a lot of things. Even walking out of the hospital into the bright summer sunshine had flooded me with anxiety. I hadn't been able to drive for seven months.

I shift into gear and press the accelerator. The engine rattles as I guide the car through downtown. Harbor Street leads out of Castille and then forks off into either the back-roads, which I took from the train station, or the Highway 16 on-ramp.

My pulse increases. I choose the on-ramp.

Finding some comfort in the fact that not a single cloud is darkening the sun, I make my way south for a distance before following the road toward the west side of Castille. The highway turns into a scenic coastal route leading to the Old Mill Bridge and several camping sites and hiking trails.

My heart thumps against my ribs when the bridge comes into view. As I approach it, a heavy, disjointed *déjà vu* descends on me. *I've been here before.*

I slam on the brakes, struggling for a breath. After pulling over to the side of the road, I get out. The road curves sharply alongside the half-moon stretch of shoreline where—

Waves wash over the rocky beach and splash against the boulders jutting into the water. A few seagulls wander along the sand and fly overhead. It's peaceful, tranquil, with no hint that anything traumatic has ever happened here.

Slipping my hand into my pocket, I touch the evil-eye amulet Charlotte had given me. My shoulders tight, I cross the bridge and climb down the slope.

Mr. Danforth stated that after getting out of the vehicle, he was able to free Ms. Mays from the passenger seat and carry her approx. fifty feet from the vehicle before contacting 911.

I calculate the distance from the rock formation and find the spot where the police report said Cole had brought me. Kneeling, I press my hand to the ground as if the earth itself can tell me more about what happened that night.

But there's nothing—no sudden flash of memory, no answers, no insight. Just the waves splashing over the shore, birdsong, and the occasional car passing on the highway above.

"Josie?"

I turn, shading my eyes. Nathan is descending the slope, his police car parked at the curve. Beneath his hat, his expression is shadowed.

"I saw Vanessa's car." He makes his way over the rocks toward me. "You okay?"

"Yes." Straightening, I pull my army jacket around myself against a sudden chill of ocean air. "I just...this is the first time I've come back here."

Lines crease his forehead. "Is there a reason you wanted to?"

"I'm not sure." I manage a weak smile, fidgeting with a ring on my finger. "I guess I still have questions about what happened that night."

A cloud darkens his face. "You want to read the police reports again?"

"No. I almost have them memorized." I look back at the water, which had been seeping into the SUV at a quickening rate, tipping it farther and farther into the ocean. With my parents and—

I block the thought and turn back to Nathan. "When did you get here that night?"

"Not long after my father did." He frowns, his eyes narrowing. "Cole had already pulled you out of the car. Smoke was everywhere. He'd been afraid the SUV would flood or explode since he couldn't tell how much of it was submerged. He'd started back to get your parents and brother out when we got there. My dad stopped him so the firefighters and rescue team could go in." He pauses. "I'm guessing you still don't remember any of it?"

"No. After this long, I doubt I ever will."

"What have the doctors said?"

"Mostly that there's a lot they don't know about amnesia and how the brain works. People have recovered from amnesia after thirty years, so…" I push at a stone with my foot. "I've learned to live with not remembering, even to consider it a blessing in some ways, but being back here has brought up a lot of questions and frustration."

"That must be awful." A troubled glint appears in his eyes. "For what it's worth, we did everything we could."

"I know." I rub the back of my neck. Unease still simmers in my chest. "Is there anything else you can tell me about what happened? I mean, anything not in the police reports."

"Not really. Except…" He takes off his hat and drags a hand through his hair. "I mean, I don't want to make things worse for you."

A humorless laugh sticks in my throat. "I don't think that's possible, Nathan."

"There are some things I've always wondered about." Tension edges his jaw. "Stuff that didn't make sense to me, and then Cole…"

"What..." My mouth goes dry. "What about Cole?"

"I never told anyone because...well, an accident like that...I mean, people say and do strange things, right? It probably means nothing. But since you're..."

At his hesitation, my instincts suddenly sharpen.

I step toward him. "Nathan, what is it?"

"Cole was the only one who could tell us exactly what happened, right?" Nathan tucks his hat underneath his arm and squints at the ocean as if he's envisioning the wreck. "And from what the EMTs could determine, and what Cole said, you'd lost consciousness at the moment of impact, if not before. When my father and the EMTs were talking to him, he said you hadn't regained consciousness at all. You'd made a sound after he got you out of the car, but you hadn't spoken a word."

I nod. "I read that in the police report."

"Yeah." A frown creases his forehead. "When they started taking you to the ambulance, he went after you, like he was desperate to go with you. My dad and an EMT had to hold him back. He was obviously in shock and upset, so I told him I'd stay with you. I think that's what he was most worried about...that you might wake up and be alone. So I promised him you wouldn't be, that I'd be there. I started back to where they had you on the stretcher. As I walked away, Cole shouted, '*She can't remember.*'"

I process the revelation. "He was right. I *couldn't* remember."

"Yeah, but how did he *know* that?" Nathan spreads his hands out in frustration. "If you didn't wake up at all, didn't say a word, how did Cole know you couldn't remember anything?"

Silence falls, broken only by the sounds of the ocean and birds. Apprehension prickles the back of my mind.

"I don't know," I finally say.

"Look, it's probably nothing." Nathan shakes his head, his mouth suddenly compressing with regret. "I mean, the guy was in total shock, bleeding, devastated. He didn't need a reason for anything he said. But the statement he gave to my father was crystal-clear down to the last detail. He never deviated from anything he said that went on the official record. So for him to make a comment that didn't make sense...I don't know either. Maybe I shouldn't even have mentioned it. But with all that was going on that night, it stuck in my brain as something I didn't understand."

"Did you ever ask him about it?"

"No. I was just a rookie, and it was my dad's investigation. I never mentioned it to him either. I thought I was making a big deal out of nothing, and then the longer time passed, the less relevant it seemed. But I never forgot it."

I glance at the ocean. I've seen the pictures of the obliterated SUV, crushed into an unrecognizable mass of metal. Despite my torment and psychic scars, I've never been surprised that my brain shut down out of sheer self-preservation.

The problem is that whatever I forgot mutated into fear, phobias, and creepy artwork instead of just going away. Like my feelings for Cole never went away—they transformed in ways I still can't fully untangle.

"Thank you for being there," I say. "I didn't know you'd promised Cole you would stay with me."

"When you woke up, I told you he was okay." Nathan sets his hat back on his head. "I hoped that would ease your mind a little."

I frown. "I didn't wake up until I was in the hospital."

"You opened your eyes right before they loaded you into the ambulance," he explains. "I guess you wouldn't remember that either. I was holding your hand, and I told you you'd been in an accident, but we were taking care of you and that Cole was okay. You looked at me...I kind of thought you showed some recognition or understanding...and then you closed your eyes again."

Nathan's face looking down at me. Angular cheekbones, wide horrified eyes, blood pooling on his skin...

Not blood. The red, flashing police and emergency lights.

My chest tightens. *Is that what the images are? Pieces of my memory?*

"Come on." Nathan extends his hand. "I'll give you a police escort back to town."

I take his hand and follow him back up the hill. The haunted tours claim that ghosts still linger in places like this.

An artist friend of mine who believed in ghosts once told me that earthbound spirits hover around because they haven't yet made peace with their deaths. Or sometimes it's because they still have a task they need to complete before they pass over. Sometimes it's because the living haven't yet let them go.

All of that is silly, of course. Ghosts don't exist.

Do they?

CHAPTER 2

Josie

Though I adore making love to Cole in any position, I love it the most when he's on top of me. He pins me down with his body, pressing me into the mattress. I'm surrounded, over-powered, conquered. I can't think of anything but him—his breath on my skin, his strong hands gripping my wrists, his body inside mine.

"Harder." Gliding my hands down his smooth back, I tighten my legs around his thighs. Sweet, aching tension pools in my lower body.

His low grunt vibrates against my neck. Our skin rubs together, the friction hot and slick. I writhe beneath him, not wanting this to end even as my body pushes toward that final blissful pleasure.

"Goddamn." Letting out a long breath, he lifts himself off me.

"Don't stop."

I tug his arms to pull him back on top of me, but instead he keeps his gaze on mine. Sea-blue eyes darkened to indigo. The air crackles. I fist the bedcovers, needing to feel him in the deepest part of me.

"Cole, I'm…"

The pressure breaks. Explosions fire through me. I cry out, gripping his arms and arching off the bed. Tension cords his muscles. After slowing his pace for an instant, he sinks deep inside me with a rough shout. I will never grow tired of the sight of him above me, his whole body tightening with sensual release.

With a muttered curse, he rolls off me and flings one arm over his eyes. After catching his breath, he pulls me against him and presses a kiss to my temple.

Resting my head on his chest, I gaze at the easel in the corner of the cottage sunroom. The lamps and ceiling lights reflect in the darkened picture window like huge stars.

"I love the way we fit together." I smooth my hand over his abdomen. Our bodies are like puzzle pieces, every section locking into place. No empty places. No missing parts.

"Me too." He tugs at a lock of my hair. "You hungry?"

"I guess that means you are."

"I could eat." He kisses my shoulder and eases up to sit on the side of the bed. "We can grab something at the pier."

After showering and dressing, we turn on two industrial-strength flashlights for the walk to the Water's Edge pier. The dark isn't quite as scary with Cole at my side, my arm tucked securely in his, but I'm still relieved when we reach the docks.

"Did you ever work on a lobster boat again?" I nod toward the silent, shadowed boats waiting to be released the following morning.

"No. Haven't been on a boat in years."

"Not even for fun?"

He shakes his head. Regret rises to my chest. Right before the accident, he'd been accepted for a spot on a prestigious scientific research cruise that would not only allow him to do the work he loved but also lead to bigger opportunities for grad school and his career. He'd have had to call Professor Jamison and explain why he needed to drop out.

"Did you ever *want* to go back to marine sciences and ocean conservation?" I ask. "It was your first love."

"*You* were my first love." He shoots me a half-smile.

"Likewise." I squeeze his arm, pleasure tingling through me. "But you know what I mean. I find it hard to believe you just stopped thinking about conservation. You had it all *planned*."

"Plans change." He shrugs and shifts his gaze to the pier. "I don't regret having started Invicta at all. Back then, I'd never have imagined I'd own a company, much less a successful one."

"So you're going to just keep expanding?"

"Why wouldn't I?" He kicks a small rock off the dock and into the water. "The company didn't get to this level without a shit-load of hard work and expansion."

"What about that water booster station I heard about? Are you going to expand into the bottled water business?"

"No. We're doing research about the station because I want to build a new distillery close to the spring. One of the reasons I bought Spring Hills was for Mischief Whiskey. It's a non-chilled filtered brand cut with pure spring water from the well. The mineral content and purity of the water is ideal for our products."

I glance at him. "So what about the class-action suit?"

Cole stops suddenly, expelling a breath. "Contrary to what people would have you believe, I'm not throttling the town's water supply. I have no intention of charging them for it, restricting access, or damaging the environment. I'm also not making concessions to a bunch of people who don't know the first thing about distilling processes or hydropower plants. They want to hit me with a lawsuit, fine. Won't be the first time."

Hot shame boils up inside me. I turn away, quickening my pace. Behind me, Cole mutters a curse.

"Josie."

"Forget it. It's none of my business anyway."

"I know you're disappointed." He grabs my shoulders, turning me to face him. In the dim light, his eyes glitter with hard regret. "You have no idea how much that kills me. But this is who I am. This is my company. I'm damn good at what I do. And I'm not going to change. Not even for you."

And why should he?

The question slithers into my mind, unpleasant and unwanted. We've managed to reconcile well, but we've made no plans beyond my stay here. I can't even envision a future together —the owner and CEO of a multimillion dollar liquor company and...me? An artist who's struggling all over again to find herself? I'm not at all certain our lives would fit together as easily as our bodies do.

It's one thing to have our secret little "fling" this summer, to hole up in the cottage and shut out the rest of the world, but the Josie and Cole of ten years ago no longer exists.

"I'm sorry." I press my hand to his chest, feeling his heartbeat thump against my palm. "I just hate knowing that people don't *like* you."

A smile tugs at his mouth. He brushes my hair away from my face. "As long as you like me, I'm good."

"I like you." *Too much. In ways that are starting to scare the crap out of me.*

"I like you too, Josie Bird." He kisses my nose.

I slip my arm back into his as we approach the pier. Though we've made an effort to keep our relationship discreet, I'm not terribly concerned with anyone finding out about us in the touristy pier crowd.

People wander in and out of restaurants and shops, and the carnival rides spin and whirl with their colorful twinkling lights and happily screaming revelers. We go into McGinty's, one of our old hangouts.

Elvis's "Hound Dog" blares from a jukebox, fishermen and

dockworkers sit at the bar, and the smells of fried fish and beer hang in the air. Cole gestures to an empty table by the wall, tugging one of the chairs away from the table for me.

"I'll grab us a couple of beers." He walks to the bar.

I pull off my jacket and drape it over an empty chair. The back of my neck prickles. I glance over my shoulder at a group of men seated near the jukebox. They're laughing and talking loudly, and their table is cluttered with beer bottles and plastic baskets of food. One of them is looking at me, a suspicious gleam in his eyes. Turning away, I'm relieved to see Cole returning.

"Pilsner okay?" He plants two bottles on the table and sits across from me.

"Sure. Thanks."

We order fried clams and onion rings, both of which make me groan with appreciation. I'd forgotten just how many little things I've missed about Castille.

Forgotten.

My chest tenses again. I feel like I'm pulling at the loose thread of a mystery. One hard tug and the whole thing could unravel—leaving me with a mess of tangled knots.

When I first decided to return to Castille, one of my goals was to say goodbye to the past. To look toward the future. And now I'm finally in a good place—enjoying painting the mural, reconciled with both my sister and Cole, part of this community again. I haven't had a nightmare or a creepy hallucination in days.

So why don't I just leave the damned thread alone?

"News flash." In an attempt to divert my thoughts, I glance at Cole with a lift of my eyebrows. "Vanessa went out with Nathan Peterson. He had a crush on her in high school and still seemed interested, so I did a bit of matchmaking. Looks like it worked."

He reaches for his beer, his mouth tightening slightly. "I meant what I said about him."

"But you're wrong. He's a good guy. He told me he'd stayed with me after the accident."

Cole's expression closes off. "When did he tell you that?"

"I went to the Old Mill Bridge yesterday." My heart bumps against my ribs. "He was passing by and saw me there."

He frowns and pushes his half-eaten food away. "And you talked to him?"

"Despite your *warning* about him, yes." Irritation snakes down my spine. "He said he'd assured you he would stay with me, since you couldn't. So how can you not think he's decent?"

"I don't trust him." He sits back and twists his neck to the side. "Why did you want to go back there anyway?"

"Well, people were visiting it on the damned haunted tours." I dunk an onion ring into a puddle of ketchup, even though I'm no longer hungry. "I wanted to see it again. See if being there would trigger any memories."

"You want to remember?" Disbelief edges his voice. "Why? I remember everything, and it's a whole other level of *nightmare*."

My stomach pitches. I stare at his hand wrapped loosely around the neck of the bottle. His fingers are square and blunt, the back of his left hand marked with a scar that hadn't been there ten years ago. His sinewed forearms are dusted with dark hair. I love scratching his arms lightly with my fingernails. Love touching every inch of his strong body.

Lifting my gaze, I catch him watching me, his expression pensive and remote. A strange tension laces his shoulders, like a vibration contained beneath his skin.

"Do you remember a keychain my dad had?" I drop the onion ring and reach for my napkin. "Teddy made it in woodshop. It was the letter B, painted blue and green."

"Yeah, I think so." He takes a swallow of beer. "Teddy also made you that carved wooden *Josie* we put on the wall of the apartment."

I nod. "But the keychain. My dad's car keys were attached to it."

"And?"

"I don't know what happened to it. You would have had it the night of the accident. Didn't you notice it?"

"I guess." He shrugs, lifting his head to meet my gaze steadily. "There was a lot going on that night, obviously. Your dad's keychain wasn't my main focus."

"I'm asking because I saw the keychain in the photo you have on the bookshelf." I crumple the napkin in my fist. "The last picture you took of us right before we left the party. How did you get that picture in the first place?"

"When I got to the hospital, I realized I still had Teddy's camera in my pocket." Cole taps his fingers impatiently on the bottle. "I was going to give it to you, but then Vanessa refused to let me see you. And I didn't know if you'd even want to see me. So I kept it, intending to get it to you at some point. Then the rumors started, and my father was pissed off...everything got so out of control that I forgot about it. I didn't find it again until a few weeks after I'd gotten to New York. And by then, I knew you didn't want any contact with me. So I downloaded the memory card contents and sent them to Vanessa. I printed that one out because...well, it was all I had left of you and your family."

"Do you remember me giving you my dad's keys?"

"I remember kissing you."

"And the keychain?"

"You gave it to me." He tilts his head back for another swallow of beer.

I let out a long breath. The constriction in my lungs eases. "We must have gotten it back, right?"

"Does it matter?" He sets the bottle on the table with a hard thunk. "Yeah, everyone wants to cling to reminders of the people we lost, but ultimately *things* don't matter. It's memories of those people and how we feel about them that matters. Hey."

He leans closer, putting his hand on my arm. "I can hear you thinking. It's really noisy."

A smile pulls at my mouth. "There's a lot going on up there."

"I know. And you should—"

A shadow suddenly falls over our table. We both look up. A burly, bearded man—the one who'd been looking at me earlier—stops beside us.

My instincts sharpen for reasons I can't discern. I sense Cole go on alert too, though there's nothing outwardly intimidating about the man. He studies Cole, his heavy eyebrows drawn together.

"Colton Danforth?"

"Yeah."

"Fuck you."

In a split-second, his fist shoots out and catches Cole square on the jaw, knocking his head back. A scream lodges in my throat. The attacker advances, landing another blow on the side of Cole's head. Cole grunts, shaking off the blow and shoving his chair back.

He rises to his full height, a bruise already darkening on his jaw. "Get the fuck away from us."

"This is for ruining people's lives, you scum." His face reddening, the man plows into him. Both men hit the floor, fists flying. Cole lands a series of punches, one of them hitting the other man's nose with a sickening crack.

"Stop it!" Jumping to my feet, I run toward them and try to push the attacker away from Cole. He doesn't budge. I'm dimly aware that the other patrons have gotten up and are gathering in a half-circle like they're watching a dog fight, but no one is doing a damn thing to stop it.

Cole has the advantage of height and muscle, but the other man is downright big and fueled by rage. They struggle, grunting and swearing, both of them landing blows. Finally Cole cracks the guy's head against the floor, stilling him for an instant.

He shoves to his feet, panting, his eyes blue fire. Blood trickles at the corner of his mouth and drips from a gash on his forehead.

I grab the back of a chair. Ice freezes my bones. *A haggard face streaked with blood, blue eyes darkened to black...*

"Fucker." Another man starts toward Cole.

The image in my head shatters. Outright fear spears through me. *Are they ganging up on him?*

"Enough!" Hank McGinty pushes his way through the crowd, his hands up. "Everyone just cool off. Danforth, you'd better leave."

Cole yanks his wallet out of his pocket and drops a fistful of bills on the table. He grabs my hand and stalks toward the door. I stumble after him, my heart still racing and my mind clouding over.

"Are you all right?" I hurry to his side when we step onto the pier.

He wipes his mouth with the back of his hand. "Fine."

"You don't look fine. Come back to the cottage."

"I'm *fine.*"

I grab tissues out of my pocket. "Do *not* be a stubborn asshole again. I've got antiseptic and ice at the cottage. God knows you shouldn't stay *here.* Those people looked as if they were about to dogpile you."

Irritation clenches his jaw, but he takes the tissues and follows me off the pier. I pull the flashlight from my backpack, and we climb the hill to the cottage. Once inside, I make him sit on the bed in the sunroom.

"I don't need nursing," he grumbles, holding his side.

"Tough shit." Turning the lamp toward him, I peer at the bruise on his jaw and a long cut along his forehead. I retrieve a first-aid kit from the bathroom and proceed to clean and bandage the cuts.

"Ow." He flinches away from the antiseptic pad.

"Don't be a baby. Hold still."

He glowers at me and sets his jaw. After taking care of his face, I push him back against the pillows and lift his shirt, wincing at the purplish-blue bruise spreading over his right side.

"You sure pissed him off." I place an ice pack against the bruise and order him to hold it there. "Did he work for Blue River Water?"

"Don't know." He shifts against the pillows with a grunt. "Probably."

"I guess you deserved his anger, then."

"Yeah."

I glance at him, widening my eyes. "*Yeah?* You're not going to defend yourself?"

He shrugs. "They're right. I put Blue River out of business. People lost their jobs. What's to defend?"

"You did it for a good reason. Why won't you tell people that?"

He doesn't respond, but a sudden fatigue descends over him, making him look ten years older. I put the first-aid kit on the nightstand and climb onto the bed beside him. He lifts his left arm and places it around me. I stroke a hand gently down his chest.

"You don't have to do it anymore, you know," I say slowly. "Pushing people away, hiding behind all your money and power, getting revenge, proving to everyone you're *not* your father…it doesn't do anyone any good. Least of all you."

He expels a heavy breath and drags a hand down his face. "Forget it, Josie."

"I won't forget it." I settle my hand on his thigh. "I have enough of forgetting, remember? There's a black hole in my memory that still haunts me. *Forgetting* is the worst thing either of us can do. If you *forget* the real Cole Danforth, then you might as well forget my parents and Teddy, Eagle Canyon, *Empire of the Gods*. The Ocean Carousel."

"I'll never forget any of that." He grabs my hips and pulls me closer. "And I'll never forget how much I loved you."

His use of the past tense elicits a sudden unease, though I

don't want to examine it too closely. I slip my hand under his T-shirt and touch the warm, hard ridges of his abdomen.

"You can still change," I tell him. "Still show people that Cole Danforth is so much more than the man people *thought* his father was. You can prove to them how much better you are."

Faint tenderness crinkles his eyes. "You want to know why I didn't want you here?"

"I'm not sure."

"Because I knew you'd get inside me again." He studies me, his hair falling over his forehead, his eyes intensely blue. "That you'd be everything good. I knew just being around you would make me want to be *better*."

"Ah." I tap my fingertips together and arch an eyebrow. "My evil plan is working."

His mouth curves. "There's nothing evil about you, Josie Bird. Only pure good."

The cracks inside me disappear, flooding me with peach-colored light. Leaning forward, I press my lips to his. At first, it's a light gentle kiss, as I'm mindful of his injuries, but then he settles one hand on the back of my neck and pulls me closer. My heartbeat increases. He urges my lips apart, sliding his tongue into my mouth in that slow, delicious way I love so much.

Before I fall into the warm haze of desire, I ease away from him. "We shouldn't do this. You're hurt."

His eyebrows snap together in a frown. "I took a couple of pansy-ass punches. I didn't get *hurt*."

I try not to roll my eyes. "Well, I'm sure a doctor would suggest you don't overexert yourself right now."

"Good thing there's no doctor in the house, then."

With that, he tilts my head up to his and claims my mouth in another kiss. My reservations go up in flames. Part of my mind is still astonished by how easily any conflict between us can fall away with the onset of passion, but it's as if our bodies remember how good we always were. He kissed me, and I fell into a swirl of pleasure. He touched me, and I flew into the stars.

The same thing happens now, except this time every kiss and touch is textured with our shared knowledge of life's swiftness. I slide my hand back under his T-shirt to his chest, relishing the sensation of his warm smooth muscles.

Still aware of his bruises, I get to my knees and press kisses across his lower lip. He tangles a hand in my hair. Heat encloses us. We fall into each other as easily as thread slipping through the eye of a needle.

CHAPTER 3

Cole

Ten Years Ago

Josie pressed her soft lips against mine. Her cherry scent enveloped me. She stroked my cheek and drew away. Reluctantly, I lifted my head and opened the front door of the Seagull Inn to usher her onto the front porch.

Chatter and laughter still drifted from the lingering guests, but the anniversary party was winding down. Benjamin Mays held his wife's raincoat out for her as she slipped her arms into the sleeves.

"Wait, I forgot something." Teddy, holding the bakery box of leftover cake, rushed back into the dining room.

"Teddy, hurry," Faith called after him. "We need to be up early tomorrow and it's twelve-thirty."

"Okay, Mom, I just need to get my tiger."

"Vanessa, make sure he does his homework." Faith looped her

coat belt and picked up the two bouquets of wildflowers I'd brought her and Josie. "He has a book report due next week for his summer class, and he hasn't started yet."

"He'll get it done." Vanessa embraced both of her parents. "Now go have a wonderful trip. Eat croissants, drink wine, gaze at priceless works of art, and don't worry about anything here. Josie will drop Teddy off at my place tomorrow, and we have a schedule for which one of us will take him to all his various activities."

"Josie made a schedule?" Behind his glasses, Ben lifted his eyebrows in surprise. "It must be the twelfth of never."

"I made the schedule, Dad." Vanessa gave him a pointed look. "Josie is just following it."

"Then it's the thirteenth of never," I said.

Ben grinned. We exchanged commiserating looks about the disheveled artist whom neither of us could love more than we already did.

"Got 'em." Teddy puffed back into the foyer with three balloon animals balanced on the cake box. "My tiger, and the balloon guy still had the bird he made for Josie. He also gave me a leftover giraffe."

"You want me to carry something?" I extended my hand.

"I'm good." Teddy wrapped his arm protectively around his cake box. "Where's my camera?"

"I have it." I held up the camera and slipped it into my pocket. "Remind me to give it to you when we get back to your house."

"Okay, everyone, hustle out." Faith shooed us all toward the door.

Ben took her hand as we walked outside to where Josie waited on the porch. A light rain fell. Streetlamps cast yellowish pools on the wet pavement.

"I got your bird." Teddy thrust the balloon, shaped into a multicolored parrot, at Josie.

"Oh, thanks. I almost forgot him."

"You did forget him," Teddy said. "I'm the one who remembered."

She tousled his hair. "Good point."

We headed down the steps, quickening our pace through the rain. Thunder rumbled. The rain came down harder. We reached the side street where Ben's SUV was parked, and he hurried ahead to open the back door.

"Sure you don't want me to drive?" I held out my hand again for the keys Josie was carrying.

"No, you've been working all day. I'll drive."

"Go ahead and take the front seat, Cole." Faith climbed into the back. "Teddy will probably fall asleep before we drive one block."

"I will not," Teddy grumbled.

Taking the cake box and balloon animals, Ben urged his son into the backseat and got in after him. I opened the driver's side door for Josie before getting into the passenger seat. We wiped a few drops of rain from our hair and faces.

"I have to take Highway 16." She handed me the balloon parrot and pulled the seat closer to the wheel so she could reach the accelerator more comfortably. "There's road construction over on Glenview, and they closed it both ways. I hope the weather's okay for the flight tomorrow."

"Radar shows a storm front moving in from the north." Ben's phone screen glowed from the backseat. "But clear after that."

After starting the ignition, Josie pulled the SUV onto the street and headed toward the road that circled the town. She turned on the media player, and the Stones' "Paint it Black" drifted from the speakers.

"When does your research cruise leave?" she asked me.

"End of July from Woods Hole. If the carnival manager won't give me time off, I'll have to quit."

"I could cover for you."

"You?"

She slanted me a narrow look. "You don't think I can staff the Milk Bottle Toss booth?"

"I know you *can*, but do you want to?"

"Sure. If I'm busy on Friday and Saturday nights, there's less chance I'll watch ahead on *Empire of Gods*. Just let me know your schedule."

I tapped the parrot's beak on her shoulder. "You're my tweetheart."

She rolled her eyes. Her mouth twitched. "Please don't."

"And being with you is parrot-dise."

"I need to break up with you now."

"Hey, your bird-day is coming up soon. Owl have to plan a special celebration for you."

"If you don't," Josie murmured, glancing in the mirror to merge onto Highway 16, "things will get a bit hawkward."

"I think I'll have to revoke my bad pun and riddle license," Ben said. "Cole is really fowling me up."

"Teddy, what was the joke you told me about the duck in the candy store?" I glanced over my shoulder. Slumped against his mother's side, the boy was fast asleep, his mouth half open.

Faith gave me an *I told you* so look, amusement rising to her eyes. "Wild Horses" came through the speakers. Josie flipped the windshield wipers to a faster speed.

No other car headlights shone through the wet darkness. The highway narrowed to a two-lane road along the coast. The Old Mill Bridge sign flashed in the lights. Rain and fog obscured the ocean.

"You want me to see if I can get us tickets for a Red Sox game before Cole leaves?" Ben's phone screen glowed again. "Sam Milton is pitching great this year. Might have a no-hitter before the season is up."

"Baseball and lobster rolls, I'm there." Josie leaned forward slightly to peer through the windshield. Her hands tightened on the wheel.

"Hey, pull over," I said. "I'll drive."

"No, it's okay. I just didn't expect it to start raining so hard."

"Looks like Fenway has a few new concessions this year," Ben reported. "There's a jalapeño cheddar burger that looks—"

The car skidded, tires screeching. Josie gasped. Alarm jolted through me. I shot a hand toward the wheel. My vision blurred. The car spun. Thunder roared in my ears, pierced by Faith's sudden cry.

Turn into the spin.

The order snapped in my brain. I didn't know if I said it aloud. Gripping the wheel, I fought to help Josie straighten the SUV. The car tilted. The wheel spun out of my hand. Ben shouted. The entire vehicle went airborne and stilled. A bird in flight.

In that suspended instant, a thousand thoughts raced through my head. *It'll be okay. We'll land safely. The car will—*

We hit the ground with bone-jarring impact. Faith's cry became a scream. Time slowed to a crawl. I grabbed the safety bar and reached for Josie. Couldn't grab hold of her, couldn't get my bearings. She was so close, right beside me, and I couldn't touch her.

The SUV slid down the cliff toward the shore, tires bouncing over rocks and sand before it flipped and rolled.

"No no no!" Ben's yell.

The ocean. The fucking...if we don't stop, we'll go under.

Metal crunched. Glass shattered. The world twisted into chaos. Pain speared through me.

Josie? Josie!

Smoke and the acrid stench of gasoline filled the interior. My head hit the side window. The back of the car slammed against the rocks, wrenching me against the seatbelt. The air bags exploded.

Everything stopped. I couldn't see. Couldn't breathe.

Am I alive? Dead? I clawed at my chest. My heart jackhammered. Smoke burned my lungs. A hissing, spitting noise came from the engine, as if the devil himself were inside. *Is that fire? Is the car going to explode?*

Josie. Ben. Faith. Teddy.

Coughing, I fumbled for the pocket on the door to find the flashlight Ben kept there. *In case of emergency.*

I couldn't hear past the hissing. Blood and sweat dripped down my face. Icy water covered my shoes, seeping up to my ankles. Beneath the smoke, I caught the smell of salt. The ocean. *If the car doesn't explode, we'll drown.*

I wiped blood from my eyes and shone the light toward Josie. She was slumped with her head against the steering wheel, her eyes closed.

God in heaven, no.

"Josie." My voice cracked like metal. I fumbled to unbuckle my seatbelt and turn toward her. *"Josie."*

She was still as death, her face drained of all color, but in the dim light her eyelashes fluttered. I looked into the backseat. Everything inside me splintered into a thousand pieces.

Teddy was on the floor, his neck twisted at an unnatural angle. His mother lay collapsed like a rag doll over him, her limbs askew. Blood was everywhere, splattered like paint. Ben was crushed forward into the passenger seat, the rear windshield shattered behind him. A rod of metal speared his chest.

Rain came through the broken window.

They're dead.

The cold, clinical statement appeared in my mind.

Get Josie out of the car.

Panic fired. I shoved at the crumpled passenger side door. It didn't move. The stench of gas grew stronger. *How far into the ocean are we? Could the car explode?*

Bracing myself, I pushed the door with my feet. It yielded halfway. I squeezed out, landing in a foot of ocean water. I stumbled to the driver's side. Shards of glass clung to the window frame. Plunging my hand through, I opened the door and yanked at Josie's seatbelt. It was stuck.

Shit shit shit.

The car tipped. Water rushed into the demolished doors. If the gas tank didn't explode, the ocean would submerge the whole car before long. I struggled to get Josie out, wrenching the seatbelt until it yielded just enough. Some distant part of my brain told me I shouldn't be moving her, I could be hurting her worse, but I had no choice.

I hauled her out. She was cold, her body limp and lifeless. I staggered to the shore. Away from the spray of the ocean, the rain lessened.

Please please please...

I sank to the ground, clutching her against my chest. Terror burned through my veins.

"Josie."

A moan, barely audible, came from her throat. I had to call 911. I had to get the others out of the car. I grabbed my cell phone from my pocket and managed to connect to emergency. I stammered out what I could.

Cole Danforth...there's been an accident...Highway 16, just past the Old Mill Bridge. Blue SUV belonging to Benjamin Mays...yes, she's still breathing...they're trapped in the car...

"Cole, stay on the line with me," the operator said firmly.

I wiped my arm over my face. Blood and rain. Smoke billowed from the engine. I had to get back there. Pulling off my soaked suit jacket, I lay it over Josie and started back to the car.

Sirens split the air. I stumbled and fell to my knees. Fought to pull air into my constricted lungs. Red lights flashed. Ambulance, fire trucks, police cars. Shouting. Intercoms crackling.

"Cole!" Henry Peterson, the police chief who was poker buddies with my father, grabbed my shoulders. "Come on, son."

Yanking myself away from him, I tried to crawl. My hands slipped on the slimy rocks. My chest ached.

"We need to take a look at you, Cole." An EMT stopped in front of me. "Just stay still."

"I'm fine. I'm *fine*. Josie..."

"We're taking care of her."

A sudden bright light flooded the beach. I sank back onto a rock and stared. Cold iced my bones. The SUV was half-submerged, waves pushing against the sides, water still seeping through the doors and windows. Officers and firefighters swarmed around the destroyed vehicle, using hydraulic cutters and spreaders to free Teddy, Faith, and Ben. A controlled frenzy lit in the air, voices rising, commands snapping.

Shoving away the EMT's arm, I struggled to get back to Josie. Two other medics were loading her onto a stretcher. Her face was bleached of all color except for streams of blood.

"*No.*"

Panic flooded me again. I lunged toward her. My fingers touched her bare leg, bloody and bruised under her torn red dress. Henry Peterson's big hand closed around my arm. Tears and rage blinded me.

"Hold on there, son." Chief Peterson forced me backward. The EMT gripped my left arm. "They'll take care of her."

My teeth chattered. "I n-need to be with her...Josie, please don't..."

"I'll stay with her." A younger man clamped his hand on my shoulder, lowering his head to look steadily into my eyes, like he needed me to trust him. Nathan Peterson, the police chief's son. When had he become an officer? The odd thought surface past my shock.

"I'll stay with her, Cole, okay?" He tightened his grip on me. "She won't be alone."

"Please." The word tasted like blood.

"I'll stay with her." Releasing me, he started toward the stretcher.

Dizziness hit me. Nausea curdled in my gut.

"She can't remember!" I shouted.

Nathan turned, meeting my gaze for an instant. The spinning red siren lights flowed on his face. He nodded swiftly, then ran toward the ambulance where they were taking Josie.

The EMT put a blanket around me. "Cole, we need to get you out of the rain."

He walked me to another ambulance. An eternity passed while he gave me oxygen and assessed my injuries. Chills rattled through me. Sweat ran down my back. I couldn't grab a coherent thought.

Chief Peterson approached and crouched in front of me. He pulled a pencil from behind his ear.

"Son, can you tell me what happened?" His forehead creased. "What do you remember?"

"The car skidded on the curve." I ran a shaking hand over my jaw. "Just after the bridge."

"Who was driving?"

I looked past him at the SUV. Officers still swarmed around it, taking notes, photos, measurements. Three EMTs were zipping up three body bags.

Darkness eclipsed my heart. I couldn't breathe. Waves rolled past the half-submerged vehicle, splashing over the rocks.

An object, wet and covered with sand, pushed up onto the shore like a beached sea creature. Red and yellow, white laces… one of Teddy's sneakers.

Pain splintered inside me, cracked me apart.

"I…I was driving."

Two EMTs picked up the smallest body bag and started toward the ambulance.

A howling noise filled the air, deep and terrible, an animal on the verge of death.

Not until Chief Peterson landed a heavy, steadying grip on my shoulder did I realize the sound was coming from me.

CHAPTER 4

Cole

Present

W hy did she go to the accident site? Why is she thinking about the keychain? What the fuck else did Peterson tell her? What does he know?

After grabbing my briefcase, I leave my office at the Invicta Spirits industrial park and stride toward the parking lot. It's not even four in the afternoon yet, but I need to get back to Castille. Back to Josie.

"Mr. Danforth. Mr. Danforth!"

I stop. A young man rushes toward me, his tie askew and eyes bright. I recognize him as a reporter who'd been at the launch party for Mischief Whiskey.

"How'd you get on the premises?" I eye his authorization badge, printed with the name Billy Grant.

Billy. *What is he—ten?*

"I'm doing a story about the rise in small-batch scotch brands." He squints at me. "Whoa. How'd you get that bruise on your face?"

"I beat up an overeager reporter."

His mouth drops open.

"What do you want?" I ask impatiently.

"I wanted to ask you about the new distillery you're building over by Spring Hills." Billy jerks his thumb in the vague direction of the spring. "One that'll use a hydropower plant to generate renewable energy. First of its kind, right?"

I narrow my eyes. "Where did you hear that?"

"I saw the permit. I also saw the records that you're testing the water in a dozen aquifers from Castille to Fernsdown. Is there a reason for that?"

"Testing is done to ensure the purity of the water. I won't put out a product that's anything less than one-hundred percent pure."

"When I talked to you at the launch party, you said you wanted to keep Invicta on the cutting edge of technology. Is that the case with the new distillery? Are you using new technologies for carbon reduction and environmental sustainability?"

"We're still in the research stages. And if you want an interview, you need to contact the press office."

He holds up his hands. "Okay, sorry. I just think it's super cool, what you're doing. I've always been into bioenergy sources. I know you're using wind power for your distillery over in Clement, but I haven't heard of hydropower being used yet. What kind of water turbines are you researching?"

Although this kid is in his early twenties, he looks impossibly young. Eager. Like he thinks he can change the world for the better.

I pull out a business card and hand it to him. "I'll give you a fifteen-minute interview about the new distillery later this week."

"Really?" His eyes widen. "Wow. Thanks."

"Call my assistant to set it up." I turn away. "Fifteen minutes. Be prepared."

I drive back to Castille, stopping at home to shower and change before going to Watercolor Cottage. While I'll take Josie wherever I can get her, I'd rather be with her at the cottage than anywhere else. Reminds me of our cramped apartment where we were always bumping into each other and never had enough room.

As both a girl and an artist, Josie came with *stuff*. Hair bands. Fuzzy socks. Premium pastels. A thousand tubes of lip balm. I loved her stuff because I loved her. But I'd also been baffled by her inability to hang up a sweatshirt.

Her cottage isn't any neater, which is just one reason I like it there. She doesn't answer my knock. I unlock the door and let myself in.

She's sprawled on the bed in the sunroom, her body moving with quick, shallow breaths indicating a restless sleep. One shapely leg rests over a pillow, and her T-shirt is pulled up far enough to reveal the curve of her ass encased in panties printed with purple butterflies.

Much as I love the sight of her, I dislike her insomnia, the way she sleeps in fits and starts. Though I haven't seen evidence of a nightmare, that doesn't mean she's not still having them. And going back to the accident site...

My chest tightens. I sit in a chair by the window and rub a hand over the back of my neck.

Two weeks. That's it. Then she's gone. After that...hell, you don't have to think about after. You just need to make sure the truth stays locked down. That means keeping her away from Peterson and any reminders of the accident.

Or *taking* her away.

A roll of half-opened Lifesavers rests on the windowsill. Peeling it open, I find a red one and stick it in my mouth. Sugar and cherry spill over my tongue.

"You're going to pay for that." Her sleep-husky voice draws my attention.

She's watching me, her arms around a pillow.

"I'll share." I push to my feet.

"You'd better."

After crossing the room in three strides, I sink onto the bed beside her and lower my mouth to hers. Though I had every intention of talking to her first, her kiss fires me with heat. The tension in my chest loosens. I brush her silky hair back from her face and slide my hand over her cheek. Breathe in her strawberry smell.

She flicks her tongue into my mouth and over the cherry candy. After passing it to her, I lower her back onto the bed. I cup her breasts and rub my thumbs over her nipples, urging them to tighten. Josie sighs, hooking her legs around my thighs and wiggling her hips against me.

"You need to stop wearing jeans when you're here." She pushes me away and rises up to unbutton my jeans and shove them off. "Makes it hard for this spontaneous sex thing we've got going on."

"I'm always hard for this spontaneous sex thing." I shed my clothes before climbing on top of her again. Nuzzling my nose into her neck, I lick the hot hollow of her throat. I fucking love that tender little spot where her pulse beats so fast.

I inch my hand under her shirt, pulling it up far enough to expose her breasts. The sight of her naked body jerks my cock into full hardness.

"God, Cole." She shifts, urging me closer and parting her cherry-red lips. "Put it in my mouth."

"Not this time." I bend to kiss her breasts, easing her underwear off her legs. As I move lower on the bed, I push her thighs open.

She rises to her elbows, her eyes widening. "Cole..."

When we first got together, it had taken her a long time to let me go down on her. No matter how aroused she was or how careful I was, she'd tense up and get self-conscious about being so exposed. But we'd both persisted, and she'd soon learned to love the act.

I pause, stroking her bare thighs. "You okay?"

A flush rises to her cheeks. She covers her face with her hands.

"Hey." Wary, I lean forward to grab her wrist. "If you don't want me to, I won't."

"It's not that." She peeks at me from under her spread fingers. "It's just that…um, no one's done that to me in a very long time."

A strange feeling fills me. "How long?"

"Since…well, since you." She clamps her hands over her face again. "This is so embarrassing."

"You're serious?" I sink back on to my heels. Tender affection weakens every part of me. Much as I hate thinking of another guy getting anywhere near Josie, I haven't been stupid enough to think she hasn't had boyfriends over the past decade.

"I never wanted another guy to do that to me." She finally peels her hands away from her face and meets my gaze, her green eyes so totally guileless that my chest aches with love.

"I haven't.." She pauses and swallows. "I haven't had a ton of boyfriends, but the ones who…well, I didn't let them do that. I guess I kind of felt like you were still the only one who sort of… deserved it?"

A laugh bursts out of me. "Ah, honey. *Deserving it* is my greatest honor."

She smiles, her face still flushed. I rub my palms slowly over her soft thighs again.

"So may I have the honor?" I ask.

She nods, her gaze fixed on mine. Despite the concession, her body is tense. I keep stroking her. She shifts her hips as her muscles begin to relax and her legs part.

Lowering myself again, I spread her open with my fingers.

She's trembling. Forcing myself to go slow, I lick her gently up one side and down the other. Josie gasps and grips my hair.

"Oh, Cole..." She starts panting, fisting her hand harder into my hair. "*God*, I forgot how good this feels. How good *you* feel."

I never forgot how good she tastes. I could lie here for hours, devouring her. I keep going, working her in all the ways I remember she'd loved. She tenses up again, but in a good way this time. I feel her urgency climbing higher and higher.

"Come on, honey." I lift my head only long enough to speak.

She has a sweet spot under her clit, and one flick of my tongue followed by a sharp arch of her hips tells me it's just as sensitive now as it was ten years ago.

"Cole, I...ah...ah!" With a cry, she bucks halfway off the bed.

Her vibrations are so hard that I force myself to count to ten to regain a small semblance of control. Only when she starts to calm do I pull myself away from her and sit up. She's flushed and sweaty. Her dazed eyes meet mine.

"You are so good at that," she whispers.

I crawl over her body and crush her mouth with mine, edging my body between her legs. She's so ready, so wet, that I slide into her with no resistance at all.

Our gazes meet. Heat and something else—something dark and almost desperate—passes between us. I grip her wrists and pin her hands to the bed before I start to thrust.

Mindless urgency takes over. My whole body drives into the need to take her, claim her. She clutches my arms, sinking her teeth into my shoulder. Some part of my brain thinks I should be gentle, but with her throaty little cries filling my head, her body tightening around mine...any self-control I have disappears like smoke.

"Now," she gasps. "Again...oh, God, *yes.*"

I can't wait any longer. The sensation of her convulsing blinds me with need. I let go with the force of an explosion, a groan tearing from my chest. I fall on top of her. The air fills with the sound of our combined breath.

The world slowly comes back into focus. Aware that I'm crushing her, I roll to the side. She exhales and sprawls her body half over mine, skimming her hand across my sweaty chest.

I close my eyes. Imagine *this,* only the two of us, as the future. All I have to do is take her away. A new start.

"Hey." Opening my eyes, I twist a strand of her hair around my finger. "How about we get away from here for a while?"

"Like where?" She props her chin on her fist and studies me. "Boston?"

"No, I mean *away.* I've got a property down in the Bahamas and a couple of…"

I stop. Her eyes cloud over. *Shit.*

"I didn't mean that to brag." I push to my elbow, willing her to believe me. "I just want to get out of here. Be alone with you somewhere *else.*"

She bites down on her lower lip. "You mean you want to go right now?"

"Yeah. I can have a plane ready…I mean, we can leave tonight, if you want to. We'll go for a couple of weeks, even a month. Anywhere you want."

"Cole, that's an incredible offer, but—"

"But nothing." My heart thumps against my ribs. "You don't even have to think about it. All you have to do is say yes."

"I can't go away with you right now." She slides her hand to the back of my neck and presses her forehead to mine. "I mean, it's a wonderful idea and I'd love to go away with you *one day*, but I'm on a deadline with the mural, and I can't leave Vanessa. Thank you so much for the offer. Can I take a raincheck?"

"Yeah." I swallow past a sudden tightness in my throat. "Sure."

"Good." She smiles and kisses me. "Maybe we can take a look at your wall map before we decide where to go."

I sink back against the pillow. Outside the window, boats dot the waters of the cove, several streaming back from the ocean after a day away.

Josie nestles up against my side. I wrap my arm around her, tugging her as close as I can. Ten years ago, I'd taken it for granted every time she tucked herself against me. We had a life-time in front of us. There would never be a day when Josie didn't curl up her gorgeous body beside mine.

What an ass I was not to treasure every goddamn time we could lie in bed together, loose-limbed with satisfaction, and just be. Not once did unease simmer through me. Not once did I feel like the ground was about to crack under our feet.

Not once was I scared of *what if?*

Not until now.

CHAPTER 5

Josie

A raincheck. To wherever I want to go in the world. I'm not sure whether the idea is more thrilling or nerve-wracking. Ten years ago, Cole and I had grand, youthful plans to travel the world together. We'd marked out destinations on his world map and planned our itineraries. Backpacking in Switzerland. Snorkeling in Australia. Sightseeing in Paris.

But that was *before*. And while I'm not so humble that I can't anticipate the excitement of traveling with Tycoon Cole on his private jets or whatever, running away with him still doesn't answer any questions. Or solve any mysteries.

Not that I'm trying to. Too much thinking will give me a headache.

Wiping my hands on a rag, I step back to study the mural. I've designed it to be read like a book, starting with the rocky cliffs and expansive land of Native Americans through the centuries—

the construction of the lighthouse and town, industrialization, the World Wars, the twenty-first century, and concluding with the Lantern Square of today.

"No one's painted the lighthouse yet," a deep male voice remarks.

I turn to find a remarkably handsome man approaching, his black hair glinting in the afternoon sunlight and his gray eyes skimming over the mural.

"No one's asked to." I toss the rag down and follow his gaze. "I've found that people are interested in painting the things they connect with personally. A lot of teachers have stopped by to paint the different schoolhouses, and students like working on Ford's College. A guy from the Parks Department stopped by yesterday to paint the woodlands, and anyone who owns one of the shops or art galleries has asked to paint their own building. Kids mostly want to paint the marine life or the other animals."

"So everyone has a personal investment in it." He glances at me with a smile. "That's pretty cool. I've never been involved with art as a community effort."

"Neither have I," I admit. "Well, not until now. Does the light-house have a personal meaning for you?"

"You could say that." He studies the white stone tower perched on the cliff, with the granite "secrets wall" lining the edge. "Though I like to think the lighthouse has a personal meaning for everyone in this town."

"It does for me." I'll never forget the day Cole was waiting for me at the lighthouse with a bag of red candy, a plush raven, and a declaration of love that set us on a path we soon thought would be lifelong.

"You're welcome to paint the lighthouse and the secrets wall, if you'd like." I extend a brush and indicate the paint cans. "I have an appointment at the library in fifteen minutes, but just leave the supplies near the storage closet and I'll take care of them later."

His eyes light with the anticipation I've seen so often in the people who stop to contribute to the wall. Never before have I thought that creating art with others—an entire community—could be so rewarding.

I walk to the library archives, where Charlotte has set aside a few more historical city maps and a detailed drawing of a nineteenth-century library. The medieval historian Professor West is at his usual table, studying another antique-looking book.

He gives me a smile of greeting, standing to move his chair when Charlotte and I pass behind him. He seems ridiculously polite in an old-fashioned, gentlemanly way. Given his dapper good looks, it's kind of cute.

I sit down and get to work examining the documents, comparing the images to the photos of the mural on my phone. I draw a few more sketches and double-check the historical changes in the street grids.

"I found another set of graphite drawings for the library that was destroyed in 1876." Charlotte brings me another stack of papers.

"I got the number of pediments and windows wrong." I show her the photo I took of my mural outline. "I think I got it mixed up with the old city hall."

"The design changed several times, so that's not surprising." She studies the picture, her brow furrowed. "Is it easy to fix?"

"Sure. You can always paint over mistakes in art."

She smiles ruefully. "Too bad it's not that easy to fix mistakes in life."

"Isn't that the truth?"

"I like the birds." She indicates the row of pigeons I painted on the balustrade of the library. "They still hang out on the balcony of the new library, so it's very authentic."

"Birds are my favorite animal. When I was a kid, I used to run around the woods looking for injured animals that needed rescuing, and I kept a particular eye out for birds."

"Did you ever find any?"

"Once I found a finch with a broken wing, and a few times I found baby birds that had fallen out of their nests." *Another time I found a sullen eleven-year-old boy who tried to convince me he wasn't lost.*

"My sister and I were talking the other day about collective nouns for birds," I tell Charlotte. "Like a kit of pigeons and a murder of crows. Do you have any resources that explain where those terms came from?"

"I can check. I'm sure there's some etymological dictionary that traces the origins."

"*The Book of St. Albans,*" Professor West says.

We both glance at him. He smiles wryly.

"Couldn't help overhearing." He gets to his feet and approaches us. "*The Book of St. Albans* is a fifteenth-century manuscript with a section on hawking and falconry. It has a list of collective nouns for animals, including birds. Also called terms of *venery.*"

"Really." I lift my eyebrows, impressed. "Does it list an unkindness of ravens?"

He nods. "And a few terms for people too. A gaggle of women, a multiplying of husbands, and an impatience of wives."

Charlotte and I exchange amused grins, both over the terms and the fact that this hunky professor is also a bit of an intellectual nerd. Or more than "a bit."

"How do you know all that?" I ask.

He slips his hands into his trouser pockets and shrugs. "I wrote a paper on medieval falconry recently and used the book as a reference. A guy who doesn't live far from here actually has one of the original texts."

"Do you need any other resources, Josie?" Charlotte steps forward to collect the drawings, her tone suddenly brisk. "City maps? Library blueprints?"

"I'll double check the mural one more time and let you know."

I write the title *Bk of St. Albans* in my notebook as a reminder to tell Vanessa about it. "And if either of you would like to paint something, please stop by. Everyone is welcome."

I say goodbye to Professor West and slip my notebook into my backpack. As Charlotte walks me to the door, I try and think of another way to befriend her without freaking her out too much. I have to approach her with quiet and caution, not unlike the way I used to creep up on wounded birds.

"How's the amulet working?" she asks.

"No curses yet." A shiver runs down my spine. I force a smile. "Hey, if you want to come and paint the mural tomorrow morning, maybe we could grab a coffee afterward. A lot of people are painting things that mean something to them personally, so if there's a building or site that you're drawn to, it's a way to make your mark."

"I'm not one for making a mark." She tugs her sweater sleeves down over her wrists and gives me another rueful smile. "But I'll stop by the mural on my way to work. I haven't seen it yet, and I've heard great things."

"Awesome. I'm usually there by nine."

Heartened by the small bit of progress, I head upstairs and return to the garden wall. The guy who painted the lighthouse did an exquisitely precise job, even shadowing the white stone with gradations of gray and black and illuminating the front with sunlight.

"Josie."

I turn at the urgent sound of Cole's voice. He's striding from the Snapdragon Inn, his expression tense.

"What?" I hurry toward him. "What's wrong?"

"Where were you?" He pushes back his cuff to glance at his watch. "You've been gone for two hours."

"I was at the library." Pressing a hand to my heart, I take a breath. "Did something happen?"

"No, but I texted you twice." The stiffness in his shoulders eases a little. "You didn't reply."

"There's no cell signal in the basement archives." I crinkle my forehead, baffled by his agitation. "You okay?"

"Yeah." He sighs and drags a hand through his hair. "Just… uh…yeah."

Stepping closer, I straighten his lapels. "Hey, do you want to paint something on the mural? There's plenty left."

"No." He glances past me to the garden wall. "You're doing great without me."

"It's a community effort." I tug on his tie. "Come on, you can paint the whale on the Ocean Carousel."

He shakes his head. "I need to get back to work."

After giving my hand a squeeze, he detaches himself from me and strides back into his office, his shoulders set. A minute later, his shadow appears in the fifth-floor window.

I return to the mural, but I can't shake a sudden disquiet. Cole has been "keeping an eye on me" from his office window, just like I often glance up to see if he's there, but if I leave, he's never before wondered where I've gone.

So why now? Where does he think I was? And why did it scare him?

❧

I've come to expect Cole at the cottage in the evenings, and it's the place where I feel the safest. After the incident at McGinty's and the uncertainty about what happens *next*, being alone with him in the messy sunroom gives me a chance to take a deep breath.

Most of the time, he spends the night, and we alternate between bouts of raw sex, fun sex, tender sex, and sometimes no sex—in which case, we curl up together and doze off.

Just like we always did before.

On Wednesday morning, the scent of coffee rouses me from a shallow sleep, as does the pressure of Cole's lips against the back of my neck. Sunlight streams through the picture window.

"You want to go for a run with me this morning?" He pats my hip under the blanket.

"Ha ha. You're funny."

"I can make pancakes instead."

"I'm interested."

He kisses my bare shoulder and returns to the kitchen. I pull myself out of bed, shoving my hair away from my face and reaching for Cole's discarded T-shirt, as has become my habit. I slip it on and shuffle into the little kitchen. He's set the wooden table with plates and hot coffee.

"Nice." I lift a mug and inhale. "Thanks."

Unlike his huge mansion, the coziness of the cottage reminds me of our shoebox apartment, where we were constantly getting in each other's way because there was so little room with both of us and all our stuff.

As I'm polishing off my first serving of pancakes, a knock sounds at the door. My spine prickles. No one ever has a reason to climb the hill to the cottage.

I start to push back my chair, but Cole gestures for me to stay seated. Instead I follow him to the entryway. He opens the door.

My heart drops. Vanessa is standing on the porch, her eyes widening.

"Vanessa." I dart between her and Cole as if I can somehow block him from sight. "What are you doing here?"

"What's *he* doing here?" Vanessa skims her hard gaze over Cole, taking in his bare chest and unfastened jeans that clearly indicate exactly what he's doing here. She snaps her attention to me. "And what the hell are *you* thinking?"

Dismay falls over me like a black cloud. "Vanessa, I can explain."

"You'd damned well better explain what you're doing with the man who killed our parents and brother."

Cole tenses, his muscles locking. I put my hand on his arm. "Give us a minute, okay?"

He hesitates. Releasing the door handle, he strides into the sunroom to pull on a shirt and shoes. He leaves the cottage, slamming the door behind him.

"Are you *kidding* me, Josie?" Vanessa tosses a large paper bag onto the sofa.

Unexpected shame boils into my chest, as if I've done something wrong. "It…we're trying to make amends."

"Make amends." Her mouth twists with derision. "Is that a new euphemism for *fucking*?"

"It's not just that." Irritation crackles through my embarrassment. "Cole and I have a long, complicated history, as you well know. So don't make me feel like I'm doing something wrong."

"I don't have to *make* you feel that way," she snaps. "Because it is wrong. Even if I could get past the fact that he murdered our family, he's an empty, morally corrupt bastard who only looks out for himself and could give a shit about anyone or anything else. He'll use you and toss you aside like an old dishrag."

"Stop it." I press a hand to my tight chest. "I don't want to hurt you, but my relationship with Cole is none of your business."

"None of my business?" She stares at me, a flush rising to her skin. "You think it won't affect me when people find out my little sister is fucking the town bad guy? The man who—"

"I know what happened," I interrupt sharply. "I know what you and everyone else think he did. I also know the truth that it was an *accident*. And I refuse to believe a bunch of crappy rumors that he was at fault. He *wasn't*."

"And you believing that makes it okay?" She spreads her arms out, her eyes flashing. "You think anything about your relationship with him is healthy? Normal? You told me you're sick of darkness and nightmares, but you're going to sleep next to *him* at night and think that will help?"

God. *Is* that what I'd thought?

"I don't expect or want him to heal me," I say. "I just want us to *settle* everything, to come to terms with what happened. To stop placing blame and stop hurting so much."

"And you have to fuck him to do that?"

"Would you stop?" Anger claws up my throat. "Cole was my best friend, the love of my life, the man I'd planned to marry one day. Not even you can reduce what we had to the crass level of *just a fuck.*"

"That's what he *was* to you." She paces to the sunroom. "He lost the right to all of that the second he drove off the goddamned road. What is he to you now?"

The question throws me. I've tried not to think too much about that, to overanalyze what Cole and I mean to each other or where we go from here.

"He's still my friend," I finally say.

"A friend you're having a summer fling with?"

My spine stiffens. "You can't belittle me about this. Nothing about Cole's and my relationship has or ever will be superficial. You know that. And I'm sorry you can't remember how much he meant to me. Did it ever occur to you that the accident traumatized him too in ways we'll never know? That he's been *destroyed* with guilt? That he's deserving of forgiveness and understanding instead of blame?"

"So that's what you're giving him?" She rolls her eyes. "How kind of you."

"My way is a hell of a lot better than suing him." I curl my hands into fists. "Did cheating Cole out of all his money bring Mom and Dad back, Vanessa? Did it make you feel better?"

"Damn right it did," she retorts. "Not to mention, it was an obvious admission of guilt."

"What the hell does that mean?"

"He caved less than a week after he was hit with the lawsuit." She spreads out her arms. "Gave me every penny without questioning a thing. Everyone knew he was terrified to go to court because he'd be proven guilty. So he went down without a fight."

"Because of *me!*" My whole body is shaking. "He didn't want me to be subpoenaed, to have to relive it. He didn't want you to have to hear about it either. He knew the only way to shut it down fast was to give you the money. Which you never should have demanded in the first place!"

"I had every right to that money. I should have asked for more."

"Right, so your lousy ex-husband could run off with it?"

The instant the words are out of my mouth, regret spears through me. This bitter acrimony is exactly what I'd wanted to avoid.

Twin spots of color appear on Vanessa's cheeks. "If you want to have an affair with that bastard, go right ahead, Josie. But I will tell you one thing."

She strides toward me. Flames fire into her blue eyes. She puts her hand on her round belly.

"You told me you want to be part of my baby's life." She takes a heavy breath. "That you want to be part of *my* life again. But if you think you can have any kind of relationship with Cole Danforth, much less an intimate one, and still be my sister and my son's aunt, then guess again. I will never let my child anywhere near a murderer or a girl who insists on sleeping with one. So you can either spread your legs for him *or* be my sister. Because there is no fucking way you can be both."

The ultimatum is a series of sharp, hard blows to my chest, robbing me of breath.

Vanessa stalks to the door, leaving it open behind her as she heads down the hill. I peer into the paper bag she'd left, which contains curtains, pillows, and a decorative clock to start furnishing the cottage.

Heartsick, I go to close the door. Cole is standing a distance away, his arms crossed and posture tense.

He lowers his arms, glancing in the direction Vanessa went before approaching me. A deep crease lines his forehead.

"You okay?"

Swallowing hard, I shake my head. He steps forward warily, as if I might shove him away, but I have neither the strength nor the desire to resist him. When he gathers me against him, I welcome the solid heat of his body, the steel-like band of his arms around me.

"I'll talk to her." He rubs his hand over my back.

"No, don't. That will make it worse. She'll never forgive you."

Tension laces through him. "She shouldn't. I don't deserve forgiveness."

"Well, you have mine. Not that you need it because I never blamed you."

He tightens his arms around me and presses a kiss to the top of my head. "I don't like where any of this is going or what it can do to you. I heard what she said."

With a groan, I lean my forehead on his chest. "I'm not going to choose between you and her."

He doesn't respond. I grip the front of his shirt.

"And don't tell me I don't have to," I whisper. "Don't tell me that whatever is going on between us will end when I leave, so I should choose Vanessa because we'll never stop being sisters. Don't tell me you'll walk away to spare me the pain of making a choice. I won't let you."

A heavy breath saws from his chest. He settles his large hand on the back of my neck. "I can't walk away from you, Josie. Not again."

I can't walk away from him either, but deep foreboding hovers over my heart. Like the thread is pulling even more, unraveling a fabric that was just starting to come together again.

"Hey." Cole slips his hand under my chin and lifts my face.

"It'll be okay. We'll figure it out. You'll be there for her, and you'll be an amazing aunt to your nephew."

Though his words are reassuring, his eyes are dark, shuttered. Unreadable. Nothing good has ever happened when I've been unable to find Cole in his blue eyes.

CHAPTER 6

Josie

The routine of painting the mural, focusing on color and design, and interacting with people who ask to help...all eases my prickliness and anxiety. The day after my confrontation with Vanessa, I repaint the mistakes I'd made on the façade of the old library and label the street signs from the nineteenth-century town map. At the very least, I've rediscovered my love of painting again in this creation of something *good*.

"Josie? Do you have a minute?"

"Sure." I turn from the mural to find Allegra King and the art historian Eve Perrin both standing nearby. After setting my paintbrush down, I grab a rag to wipe my hands. "How can I help you?"

"Eve and I have been looking ahead to the different projects we want for the new Arts Center," Allegra explains. "Construction will be finished this fall, and we want to hit the ground running. We'd like to ask if you'd be interested in being on our recruitment committee when we start hiring teachers."

I blink. "Seriously?"

Eve smiles. "Seriously. It would mean reviewing applications, making recommendations, offering input. You can do it all from California. Since you've made the mural such a collaborative effort, we're especially interested in your ideas for community-based art projects."

"Well, people painting this mural was kind of an accident." I rub my hands on my overalls, both flattered and uncertain about their proposition. "I hadn't intended for it to be a collaborative effort. It just turned out that way."

"Exactly." Allegra nods, a pleased smile crossing her face. "You have a knack for involving people in art, which is why we want your input."

"We know you'll be busy when you go home," Eve adds. "But if you'd consider this as a part-time position, we'd love to have you on the committee. We'll find more time to talk about it before you leave."

Pleased at the idea of having an influence on the Arts Center, I thank them and promise to let them know. As I return to the mural, Eve's remark about *leaving* sticks in my head.

What if I stay?

Not once in ten years have I considered moving back to Castille. I've built a life for myself in San Francisco, even if it has been populated by darkness and nightmares.

But what if I did move back? What if I could stay here and watch my nephew grow up? What if Cole and I really could manage to turn our relationship into something long-lasting again?

The questions flutter like fireflies through my mind. I can't imagine any of the answers fitting together properly. If my sister has anything to say about it, watching her son grow up precludes any hope of a relationship with Cole.

Too many broken pieces.

When the afternoon light begins to wane, I pack up my supplies and walk to the house on Poppy Lane. Upset as I've been with Vanessa, I can understand the root of her anger, even if it's misdirected at Cole. I might not be able to remember anything, but Vanessa remembers too much.

She'd taken the horrific phone call from the police, been forced to identify the bodies, held me in the hospital while she told me what had happened. In the midst of her own shock and grief, she'd made the funeral arrangements, kept Cole away from me, dealt with paperwork, bills, all the horrible, mundane details of which I was oblivious. In the process, her devastation twisted into hatred of the only person she could blame.

But still...there has to be room for forgiveness. *Somehow.*

Bracing myself, I ring the doorbell. Vanessa opens the door, her rounded figure draped in a pink flowy blouse and black cropped pants.

She glances behind me. Her eyes narrow. "Are you alone?"

"Yes. We need to talk."

She pulls the door open wider to let me into the foyer. "If you're planning on being with *him*, there's nothing to talk about."

"And you and I aren't going to get anywhere if you issue me an ultimatum like that." I set my backpack down and step closer to her. "Do you really think Mom and Dad would want you and me to fight like this? Again?"

Her eyes meet mine for an instant, but then her jaw stiffens. "Do you really think they'd want you to be with the man who killed them?"

"They would *not* blame Cole or think of him that way. And if you think they would, you're wrong. You know that. He did everything he could to correct course. I truly hope you and I can do the same thing now."

"What is it you want, Josie?" Irritation flashes over her expression. "Family dinners with you, me, and Cole Danforth? Whatever you have going on with him, I want no part of it. I don't want my son to be part of it either. I'm sorry, but it's pretty fucked up."

My chest clenches. "No, it's not."

"*Everyone* will agree with me," she says. "It's like some twisted version of the Stockholm Syndrome."

"Oh, stop it. I don't care what *everyone* will think. That was the night Mom, Dad, and Teddy died, and it was the night Cole and I *survived*. I don't care what people *or* you have said about him. The fact is that he did nothing wrong. In fact, he saved me. Nathan said Cole had gotten me out of the car because it was getting submerged. There's no telling what could have happened."

"Does what *could have happened* even matter?" Vanessa puts her hands up in exasperation. "None of it *would* have happened if he'd been careful."

"It was a horrible accident. No one is to blame, least of all Cole."

"Look." She leans closer, her features hardening. "Putting that aside, what about all the crap he's pulling with his company? Screwing people over, shutting down smaller businesses, generally being an asshole? Is that the kind of man you really want to be with?"

"You don't know the whole story or the truth. No one does."

"I don't care either. The evidence speaks for itself, both then and now. I will never accept you and him together."

The ache inside me deepens. I hadn't expected to change her mind in five minutes, but ten years ago she'd been the one to give me advice on how to get Cole's romantic attention. Now she can't bear the thought of him in my life.

"Look, I don't have time for this right now." She glances at her watch. "I have to go. An old friend from high school contacted me asking if I can help with redecorating her living room, so I told her I'd stop by."

"That's great." Even though I can't stand fighting, I'm pleased at the idea of her rediscovering her talent like I've done with mine. "You were always so good at that."

Her mouth twists with self-derision. "Something to do, anyway."

"I also stopped by to clear out some of the stuff in the basement." I gesture toward the basement door. "I talked to Dad's friends at the Historical Society, and they're interested in his book collection for their library."

"Go ahead." She grabs her purse and car keys from the table. "Just lock up after you leave."

She goes out to her car. I head down to the basement, flicking on the lights.

I tackle the organization systematically, setting my father's belongings in one corner and my mother's artwork in another. Books, paintings, clay pots, notepads, old palettes. A set of framed paintings leaning against the wall yields one of my favorite Faith Mays series—*Interiors*, in which she studied the realistic effects of light.

Setting them aside to take back to the cottage, I turn toward another stack of boxes labeled with my name. Inside the first box is a pile of drawing pads. I open the first one.

Cole's face, ten years younger and captured perfectly in time, gazes back at me. Strikingly intense eyes beneath dark brows, high cheekbones slanting toward his strong jaw and beautiful mouth with the notch just below his lower lip. The pencil drawing almost vibrates with youthful energy, every detail from the strands of his burnished hair to the dusting of stubble on his face lovingly depicted.

The entire drawing pad contains sketches of him. I don't even remember creating so many images of Cole, though I'm not surprised. Everything about him, from the way light fell across his hair to the flex and pull of his muscles, was art in motion. Hardly a wonder that I found him such a source of inspiration.

My phone buzzes with a text.

COLE: Are you at home?
JOSIE: I'm at the house on Poppy Lane. You still at work?
COLE: Yeah. You want to go on a date with me?

I smile.

JOSIE: About time you asked. Yes.
COLE: Can I pick you up there or do you want to meet me?
JOSIE: I'm alone. You can pick me up.
COLE: Be there in ten minutes.

After setting the phone down, I continue unpacking boxes until the doorbell rings. I let Cole in and indicate my dusty overalls with a grimace.

"Depending on where you're taking me, I need to change."

"We can stop at the cottage first." He leans in to kiss me. "What're you doing here?"

"Sorting through the basement." Gesturing for him to follow me, I descend the stairs again. "It's not only Mom and Dad's stuff, but mine too. I just found a whole sketchbook of drawings I once did of you."

"What are you going to do with it all?" He picks up a framed painting of an intricate, tangled forest lit by hundreds of lanterns.

"Donate some of it." I set another one of my boxes against the wall. "I guess I'll get rid of a lot of my old stuff, except my artwork of course."

"You ever think of doing a solo show of your older paintings?" He sets the painting down and picks up another one.

"Not really. I've tried painting forests and animals again, but they never come out right. I still haven't figured out what my new aesthetic is."

"You've definitely hit a stride with the mural."

I heft a few more boxes to the side as a reminder to sort through them tomorrow. Behind the stack, pushed into a corner, is a legal box labelled MAYS in an unfamiliar penmanship. I pick it up and start to set it with the others when I notice the police label on the other side.

My heart stutters.

"What's wrong?" Cole comes to my side, his eyebrows drawing together.

"This is a police box. It must be the stuff from the SUV."

He tenses. "Josie, leave it alone."

I tighten my grip on the box and look at him. His expression is shuttered.

"I can't."

Cole steps away, tugging a hand through his hair. "You came here to do something good. And you're succeeding. So how is digging into the past *good?*"

"Because maybe sometimes it provides light." I set the box on a table and take hold of the lid.

Anxiety twists through me. I pull the lid off the box. My first glance at the contents steals my breath—my mother's purse, a *Garfield* book that had belonged to Teddy, my father's wallet, a handful of Lego mini-figures, the SUV manual, several pens, the garage door opener.

And there, at the bottom, the wooden letter B attached to my father's keys. The edges are splintered, the paint dirty and peeling, but it's still intact. I close my fingers around it. Shock flares through me.

"Hold on, they're in my coat pocket." My father pulled his raincoat *from the restaurant's front closet and dug into one of the pockets. He took out the keychain and handed it to me.* "Thanks."

"Sure. Cole and I are staying over at your house tonight, if that's okay. Easier to get you to the airport in the morning."

"I'll drive." Cole stopped beside me and extended his hand for the *keys.*

My brain rebels, shutting off as if I've yanked out an electrical plug. A sick feeling rises to my throat. I take the keychain out of the box and lift my gaze to Cole.

He's watching me, his features set and his eyes starting to burn with…what? Fear? Anger?

"I…" My mouth goes dry. "Did I give you the keys?"

He crosses his arms, the lines of his body tensing. A muscle ticks in his jaw.

"Cole."

"You always let me drive."

"Cole." Panic brews in my gut, flickering into my veins like the start of a firestorm. "Don't do this to me. I can't *remember*. You're the only person still alive who was there. I had a…I think the hallucinations I've been having are somehow related to my memory, that I'm…"

His expression darkens. "What?"

"I think I'm remembering stuff, but I can't be sure. I thought going back to the accident site might trigger *something.*"

"Did it?"

"No." I grip the keychain tighter, my panic intensifying. "But when I was about to cross the bridge, I had a weird sense of *déjà vu*, like I'd been there before. Which of course I have, but I…I felt like it was related to *that night.*"

Cole studies me for a long time, his guard so thick I can't read anything in his expression—no sorrow, no regret, no anger. It's like he's locked himself behind a door to keep me out.

Oh, no. I can't let him do this again. I can't lose him again.

"I need to know." Pressing my hands to my face, I close my eyes and take a deep breath. "I *need to know* what I'm missing or I swear I'll go insane. This…this empty space in my memory isn't a harmless void where everything just disappears. It's a fucking *well*, the deepest, darkest well you can imagine.

"And for the past ten years, horrible, creepy things have grown out of this well. Phobias, nightmares, anxiety, resentment. I need it to stop. And the *only way* I know of to make it stop is to fill the well with the truth. But nothing has worked—therapy, medication, fucking acupuncture. I don't know what else to do, and *you* are the only person who can help me. You're the only one who was there. The only one who has the goddamned key."

I lower my trembling hands and force my gaze back to him. My heart slams against my ribs.

He's so tense he looks as if he's about to crack, his mouth compressed and his eyes glittering. The color is gone from his face, leaving his eyes a bright, shocking blue.

"God, Josie." His voice is raspy, shaking. "I'm so fucking sorry."

I grab the back of a chair. My legs weaken. *"Cole?"*

The words break from his throat like shattering glass.

"You never gave me the keys."

CHAPTER 7

Josie

The world spins, tipping me into the black, gaping well that has been hovering at my feet for years. Darkness engulfs me.

"No, it's okay." I stood on tiptoe to kiss Cole's cheek, inhaling the citrus scent of him. "I'll drive."

I'll drive. I *drove.*

I. Was. Driving.

Nausea chokes my throat, filling my mouth with bile.

"Josie…" Cole starts toward me.

I surge past him to the stairs, running to the open door of the bathroom. My knees crack against the tile floor. I retch into the toilet, my insides churning and my mind crushing beneath the weight of the truth.

"Josie, please…" He closes his hands around my shoulders, lifting me upright.

"Oh, my God." I wipe my mouth with the back of my hand,

struggling for the strength to stand. I can't look at him, can't bear to see whatever is burning in his eyes—anguish, regret, pain. "It was my fault. I killed them."

"*No.*" Desperation wrenches his voice. "No, Josie, please…"

"And you…" I heave a breath into my aching lungs. "You…you lied to me. You lied to everyone."

"I…I had to." He tightens his grip on me, and suddenly his close proximity is too much, too overwhelming, too intense. "I couldn't stand what knowing the truth would do to you."

She can't remember.

I grab a tissue and shove him away, stumbling to the entryway. My mind is reeling. Shards of memory tumble and crash like a kaleidoscope, discordant and chaotic.

Rain hitting the windshield. "Wild Horses." My father's voice….something about the Red Sox… A sudden skid, the steering wheel spinning out of my grip, pure terror. Cole's shout, his hand closing over the wheel.

She can't remember.

He hadn't meant I was incapable of remembering because he hadn't known I'd lost my memory. Instead his words to Nathan had been a plea, a prayer that I'd forgotten. She *can't* remember. *Please don't let her remember.*

Somewhere in the depths of my unconsciousness, had I heard him? Had my brain responded and slammed a steel door down on the previous hour, locking all the horror away? Did Cole's plea instigate the black hole in my memory?

Bile floods my throat again. I swallow it back down, fumbling to close my shaking fingers around my backpack. My insides burn.

"Josie, don't go." He grabs my wrist.

"Let go of me." I spin to face him and almost reel backward at the sight of him—face drained of color, the blazing blue of his eyes, the agony twisting his features. "This is why you left, isn't it? It wasn't because you thought I wouldn't be able to stand being near you again. You left me because you were scared I'd find out the truth."

"It was both, Josie." He strokes his thumb across the pulse pounding violently under my skin, like he's trying to soothe a terrified animal. "I left because I never wanted you to find out. I never wanted *this* to happen. And if you were anywhere near me, you'd remember what I did."

"But you *didn't* do it!" Tears spill over. "Despite what you tried to make me believe, I still wanted you. I needed you to hold me and promise me there was still light somewhere on the surface, that one day I might be able to claw my way back to it. I needed to know you were the one person in the world who wouldn't leave. And then you fucking *did*."

"I know." He pulls me closer, lowering his head and forcing me to look into his anguished eyes. "I'm sorry. I thought it had to be the right thing, the only way to protect you. I...Christ, Josie, everything was such a fucking mess...you were barely responsive, I thought the car would go under before the police got there, and with your parents and brother trapped inside...Then they took you away, and there were the fucking body bags...I lost my mind. I was terrified of what would happen to you, if you'd even survive. The only thing I could do was take the blame and hope...*pray*...everyone would believe it."

"Including me." I twist my arm, yanking myself from his grip. Sudden anger burns through my heart. "You wanted me to live with a fucking black hole in my brain. A thing that ate up everything good and spewed it back out like vomit."

"No!" He holds up his hands. "I had no idea that's what it would be like for you. I didn't know the first damned thing about memory loss...I just knew that the truth would destroy you. And the only way I could stop that from happening was to keep it from you."

"It didn't work." I stalk toward the door. "The lie destroyed me."

And the truth is crushing me to pieces.

"Josie!"

I run. His shout follows me out the door and down the front walkway. Outside, the sunlight temporarily shocks me.

Why is there sun? Shouldn't the world be covered in darkness now?

My heart jackhammers. I have to get away from him.

"Josie, stop!"

Cole's heavy footsteps echo on the porch steps. He's stronger and faster, but I'm fueled by rage and fear. Shoving open the front gate, I dart heedlessly into the street, my breath shallow. A car horn blares.

"Josie, please!"

I rush toward the pathway cutting through the woods, my singular thought one of escape. I'm vaguely aware of a jogger stopping, but tears blind me and my breath scrapes my throat, and my lungs are on fire, and my heart is broken…shattered… crushed beyond all hope of repair.

A police car turns the corner, heading in the direction of our house. Just before I reach the woods, Cole's arms close around me from behind. He hauls me back against his heaving chest.

"Josie, I'm begging you." His voice is jagged like a piece of rusted metal. "Please, *please* stop."

For an instant, so quick I barely recognize it, my instinct for *him* takes over. I collapse against his chest, let the steel strength of his arms encircle me, welcome everything I have always loved about his solid presence.

He presses his face against my hair. Shudders wrack his body.

"I'm so fucking sorry." His heart thumps heavily against my back. "If I'd known, I never would have done it. Never. But I *didn't* know. I only knew that my heart was on fire, and that I'd never stop seeing your parents trapped in the backseat or the EMTs pulling them out of the car, or the fucking body bags…and then when I found out you didn't remember, it seemed like goddamned fate that I'd done the right thing. I couldn't stand the thought of you thinking you were to blame."

"I *was* to blame!" The cry rips from my throat, high and shrill. "I drove off the road. I killed them. It was my fault."

"No. Please. No…" He tightens his arms around me. "I lied so you wouldn't tell yourself that. Because I loved you so much. I love you even more now. I've never stopped loving you, Josie, not for one second. All I wanted to do was protect you."

The confession shatters against the ice collecting around my heart. "Let go of me."

"Josie?"

Nathan's voice breaks through the screaming in my head. Cole grips me even harder, his breath rasping against my ear.

I scrub a hand across my eyes and force myself to focus on Nathan. He's getting out of his parked car, one hand on his gun and the other in the air. He shifts his gaze guardedly from me to Cole and back again.

"You need some help?" he asks.

A hysterical laugh bubbles into my throat. *What a question.*

"No." I pull myself away from Cole. Dread tenses my spine, weights my shoulders.

Nathan narrows his eyes, shifting his hand on his gun. A couple of dog-walkers on the other side of the street stop to watch the commotion, and several people have come out onto their front porches.

Cole backs up a step. I feel him watching me, sense the plea radiating from him, but I can't speak past the tightness in my throat.

"Josie, are you all right?" Nathan, his face drawn and pale with concern, approaches. "You want me to call Vanessa?"

I shake my head. Pain boils into my chest. More tears blind me.

"I have to go." I back away, putting my hands up. "Please don't call anyone. Stay away, both of you."

I turn and run.

                    ❧

I stumble up the hill to the cottage. Dark is starting to engulf the cove. Sweat trickles down my back. I turn on all the lights, but not even the blazing high-wattage bulbs provide any comfort.

Grasping a semblance of logical thought, I realize Nathan will still contact Vanessa about what he just witnessed. I hammer out a text to my sister that I'll talk to her tomorrow in the hopes that she won't come looking for me.

Pressing my hands to my eyes, I sink onto the bed. Exhaustion and grief press down on me. Now more than ever, I'm desperate to sleep, to let the sweet oblivion stop the clawing pain.

I'm sorry, Mom.

I'm sorry, Dad.

I'm sorry, Teddy.

Clutching a pillow, I curl onto the bed in a tight ball. How do I not remember any of it? The lie I've been living had made perfect sense. Mom and Dad had been drinking champagne at their anniversary party. That's why Cole was driving Dad's SUV.

I'd never questioned it. Cole was right. I always let him drive, even if we were just going to grab takeout. So why had I insisted on driving that night? Why hadn't I given him the keys when he'd asked for them?

Wait a minute. He'd been late to the party because he'd worked overtime and then he'd run into Professor Jamison, who'd offered him the research cruise position. Not only had he also worked the previous day, he'd been up since before dawn and hauled lobster traps for ten hours. Then he'd heard about the cruise and came to the party...I'd have known he was exhausted.

"No, that's okay. I'll drive."

Everything had been fine, though, right? I'd been tired, but I hadn't been drinking. I wasn't distracted. I never used my cell phone when I was driving. It hadn't even crossed my mind that I'd have trouble navigating in the storm.

We'd be at Mom and Dad's in twenty minutes. Then in the morning, we'd take them to the airport—likely with Cole driving —and send them off on their grand tour of Europe before we treated both Teddy and ourselves to breakfast at Waffle Castle. Teddy had been anticipating the Butter Pecan Special.

Why in the love of God didn't it turn out the way we'd planned?

Because you fucked up. You did something wrong.

No, I didn't! I was a good driver. I wouldn't have been speeding. I wouldn't have done anything stupid.

But what if I did?

Tears flood my eyes and spill down my cheeks. The pain will break me in half. I press my face into the pillow and pray for sleep. Just an hour or two. Anything to ease the questions stabbing my brain.

I'm sorry I'm sorry I'm sorry. Please forgive me. Please let me know you don't blame me, that you don't think it was my fault. Mom, Dad, Teddy...please.

Mom had always known there was more to this world, to life, than we can see or touch. Her paintings of mystical women radiated with otherworldliness. She'd known the curtain between here and the beyond was thin enough to be transparent, that all we had to do was pay attention, look hard enough, believe...and we'd *know.*

I'd once believed the same thing. My intricate drawings of barefoot girls walking through dense, tangled forests, finding their way with lanterns, moonlight, the help of mischievous animal companions...hadn't that all been rooted in a belief in magic and mysticism?

Please show me you forgive me. Give me a sign. Anything. A slight breeze. Mom, let me feel the brush of your hand on my hair. Dad, can I hear you laugh? Teddy, who was your favorite superhero? I can't remember.

I struggle to focus on their faces...Teddy's grin, Mom's and Dad's eyes...but the faded memories crack apart in my head. From the broken pieces, horrible images rise of them trapped in the backseat, features twisted with agony, mouths open in silent screams...

No. No. Please give me a sign that you still love me. That it didn't hurt too badly. That you're okay now, that you're together and laughing and happy again...please.

Are you there?

Dad?

Mom?

CHAPTER 8

Cole

What have I done?

The question spears through my head over and over. I haven't slept since I left Josie yesterday afternoon, and my five-mile run still isn't burning the question out of my mind.

I run faster, my shoes pounding the dirt trail, my lungs aching. Sweat rolls down my back. I push forward, even faster. I'll outrun it all—the demons, the lies, the wrong fucking choices. The clawing, piercing guilt.

Knowing what I do now about how the loss of her memory affected Josie, would I have done things differently? But what would it have done to her if she'd been told she was driving the car, and yet still didn't remember anything? Would that have made her phobias and nightmares even worse?

I'll never know. Hunched in the rain, crushed to the bone, staring at the twisted mass of the wrecked SUV, watching the EMTs cart away three body bags…

The road had forked out in front of me, neither path leading anywhere good. Lie and hope it would protect Josie. Or tell the truth and know it would devastate her.

In a split-second, I chose my path. For ten years, I've lived with it.

And now...

I don't know what the hell to do. I can no longer trust my instinct to protect her. I can't even trust myself.

You couldn't have known.

I should have known. Such a fucking asshole to think I could keep it a secret.

Knowing the truth would have destroyed her.

My lie destroyed her.

Chest heaving, I come to a halt in the middle of the woods. Sunlight falls through the trees. Birds chirp and squirrels rustle. I press a hand to a tree trunk and bend to catch my breath.

I didn't have a choice.

It wasn't your call.

Yes, it was. It was my goddamned call to do whatever the hell I needed to protect that girl from the devastating truth.

And how'd that work out for you?

Fuck.

Straightening, I wipe my face on my T-shirt sleeve.

How could I have told her the truth that night? *Ever?* How could I have told anyone? When Henry Peterson had asked me what happened, how could I have opened my mouth and said, "Josie was driving the car."

I *couldn't*. Nothing—not even torture under interrogation—could have forced me to implicate Josie in the accidental deaths of her parents and brother. Her sister's filing of the wrongful death lawsuit only cemented my belief that I'd done the right thing. What if Vanessa had known Josie was driving the car? What would *that* have done to them both?

I start back toward Lantern Square. I can't get my head

around how this happened. The keychain? Or was it whatever Nathan Peterson told Josie at the accident site? Or did it all start the second she came back to Castille?

I should have tried harder to get her to leave but I'm fucking powerless when it comes to her. A decade ago, that girl had been my every weakness. That hasn't changed. It never will.

I walk slowly back to the Snapdragon Inn and shower in my office bathroom. Then I dress in a suit and tie in a feeble attempt to reestablish some normalcy.

Outside the window, a police car pulls up in front of a coffee-house.

My insides tense. Despite my gratitude toward Nathan for staying with Josie when I couldn't, I've always known he was suspicious about that night.

At the hospital, after his father left to take a phone call, Nathan and I had been alone in the room.

"Hey, can I ask you something?" he said.

"Yeah." Every piece of me had shattered.

"What kind of car do you usually drive?"

"A Ford." I glanced at him through swollen eyes. "Why?"

He shrugged. "Just curious."

Even under the suffocating grief, my instincts had sharpened. *Stay away from him.* He was suspicious. I'd gone out of my way to avoid being alone with Nathan Peterson again.

So what had he told Josie? Had that jogged something loose in her mind? Set her on the path to finding out the horrible truth?

Too many fucking questions. No answers.

A knock sounds at the door and then my uncle enters. I groan inwardly. He's always ignored my dictate that employees need to make an appointment to see me. With him, I've always let it slide.

"You look like hell," he remarks by way of a greeting.

"Feel like it too." I grab a bottled water from the fridge and crack the lid open. "What do you want?"

"I heard there was some sort of issue over on Poppy Lane near

Josie's house." Slipping his hands into his pockets, Gerald draws his eyebrows together. "Officer Peterson was involved. You want to tell me what happened?"

"No."

"Cole."

"It's no one's business." My jaw tightens. I stare out the window at the square teeming with people. "Josie and I had an argument."

"A public one, from the sound of it. The lawyers are already frazzled. They won't like hearing that you might be up on assault charges."

"I didn't *assault* her."

"Nathan Peterson has a different view of that."

The plastic bottle crumples under my grip. "Fuck Nathan Peterson."

"Look." Gerald approaches me, his tone gentling. "You've been working your ass off on the Mischief Whiskey launch. And having Josie back in town has been rough on you. So why don't you take some time off, go to Europe or find a beach in the Bahamas where you can just do nothing. Let this situation die down and give the lawyers a chance to chillax."

"Please tell me I didn't just hear you use the word *chillax*."

"Hey, I'm hip." A brief grin pulls at his mouth before his expression sobers. "I'm also serious. You need to leave for a while."

I settle my gaze on the half-finished mural. The vibrant colors glow in the sun. A mother and her daughter, a little girl with brown pigtails, have stopped to look at it. The girl is talking animatedly, gesturing to the downtown scene.

"I'm not going anywhere," I tell Gerald.

"It's one thing for people to think you're an asshole CEO." A hard note enters his voice. "It's quite another for them to think you're capable of physically hurting a woman. And believe me, that's not a tough jump in thought for the residents of this town."

"Fuck the—"

The words break off. Fatigue hits me, like the weight of ten years has suddenly dropped onto my shoulders.

"Cole?" Gerald clamps a hand on my arm. "You okay?"

I'm not okay. I'm fucking tired.

If there is one person in this world I'd confess to, it's my uncle. But I won't.

I wasn't driving the car. Josie Mays was. She lost control at the wheel.

Nothing on this earth will make me say those words aloud to anyone.

Below the window, the pig-tailed girl at the mural finishes whatever she was talking about and grabs her mother's hand. Together they start toward the plaza. The girl skips a couple of times, a little hop of joy.

I shove Gerald's hand off my arm. "I'm fine. I'll talk to you later."

"You've got that interview in ten minutes with the kid from the *Drink Me* website."

Shit. "Cancel it."

"You're the one who agreed to it. That site is a major influencer, and you have a chance here to get them on our side." He backs toward the door, his gaze narrow. "Don't screw it up."

I drag a hand through my hair and force my brain to refocus. Maybe if I think about company strategies, I can come up with a way to fix this disaster with Josie. Or maybe I'm an asshole who doesn't know what the fuck to do next.

When Billy Grant arrives—slicked-back hair, badly knotted tie—I indicate the chair across from my desk and sit down to answer questions. Somehow I manage to compartmentalize my brain and focus.

The kid is smart and good. He's done his homework about hydropower plants, water and wind turbines, and renewable energy technologies for distilleries. I answer all his questions, though impatience simmers under my skin.

"Last question," Billy says. "Can you tell me anything about your future plans to expand Invicta Spirits?"

My chest constricts. For years, expansion has been my main goal. The research and use of new technologies and bioenergy have all been part of that goal. If I don't work on pushing Invicta past our competitors, I don't know what the hell else I'd do.

"The plan is to expand," I say.

He smiles. "Can I quote you?"

"Sure." I get to my feet and shake his hand. "Thanks for stopping by."

"Thanks for talking to me. This has been really great."

After he leaves, I sit back down and stare at the wall map, dotted with more red pins than blue.

A sudden urge seizes me with crushing force. I want to be back in the woods with Josie running after me, ponytail bobbing and red backpack bouncing. I want to lie with her on the sun-soaked rocks in Eagle Canyon, the smell of the forest mingling with the coconut scent of her sunscreen. I want to be back in our apartment, tangled in bed with her, exchanging kisses that taste like cherry Lifesavers, making her morning coffee.

I want *her*.

And I want my old self back. The young man who'd pulled himself out of the quicksand bitterness of his childhood and into something new. Hopeful. The boy who'd loved being out on the ocean. Who'd learned how to believe he was worthy of good things.

Because of her.

I pull out my cell phone and text her again. *I'm sorry. I love you.*

I stare the screen for what feels like an eternity. There's no response.

CHAPTER 9

Josie

Dawn bleeds over the horizon. I pull myself off the bed, my whole body empty and aching. For hours, nightmares blistered whatever sleep I managed to grasp. The disembodied heads transformed into full-fledged monsters that jolted me awake, sweaty and terrified.

There was no sign. No indication that my parents and Teddy are at peace. No hope of forgiveness. Just...dark and terror.

I manage to drag myself to the shower and dress in clean clothes. I don't recognize the face staring back at me in the mirror. I've become one of my horror-show paintings—skeletal, hollowed-out, bruised.

I turn on my phone. Messages scroll over the screen, some from Vanessa asking me to contact her as soon as I'm up, and others from Cole. His texts flay open my heart all over again. *I'm sorry. I love you.*

I set the phone aside without responding. *Think, Josie. What do you do next?*

I don't know. I don't know.

I stare out the window. The entire world is wavering, surreal.

The harbor and park, alive with a morning crowd, make no sense. *How can fishermen take their boats out to sea? How can people walk their dogs? How can two young mothers push baby strollers through the park?*

I squint against the sunlight. At the base of the hill, a police car is pulling into the parking lot.

Nathan.

Wrenching open the door, I hurry down the hill. He's getting out of the driver's seat, shading his eyes as I approach. Only when I get closer do I realize that Vanessa is in the passenger seat.

"*There* you are." She climbs out of the car and hurries toward me. Nathan follows, an unmistakable protectiveness radiating from him.

I slow to a walk. *How can I tell my sister? How can I not?*

She meets me on the pathway, her gaze searching my face. "Are you all right?"

"Sorry." Attempting a smile, I reach for her hand, somewhat soothed by the sensation of her cool fingers closing around mine. "I've been a little...upset."

"After what Nathan told me yesterday, and you not responding to my texts...I was getting worried." She glances over her shoulder at him and squeezes my hand. "He offered to drive me over here to check on you."

"You need me to have a word with Danforth, Josie?" he asks.

Shaking my head, I press my lips together.

Vanessa frowns. "But what did Cole do to you? Nathan said he was running after you, and you were crying...what happened?"

God in heaven. Nausea boils in my throat again.

"Josie?" Her eyes widen with alarm. "What *happened*?"

"It's not...I can't..."

"Josie!" She grabs my other hand, her tone sharpening. "*What did that bastard do to you?*"

I don't even know where to begin answering that question. I yank myself from her grip and step back.

Will I ever regain my full memory of what happened that night? Does it even matter? It's not as if my knowledge will change anything.

"Josie, I'm going to Danforth for answers." Nathan steps forward, his shoulders tensing. "He's caused enough trouble around here. I won't have him scaring you like this."

"He didn't…" I take a deep breath. The words dredge up from the dark, slimy pit of my soul. "It was me."

"What was?" Vanessa asks.

Wrapping my arms around my middle, I start shaking. "I was driving the car."

Silence. The air thickens.

"The car?" she repeats, her tone puzzled. "What car?"

"Dad's SUV." I force the confession past the knot in my throat. "The night of the accident. It wasn't Cole, Vanessa." I lift my gaze to hers. Pain spears me anew at the widening, incredulous look in her eyes. "It was me."

Nathan blinks. Vanessa stares at me, one hand on her belly. "What…what are you talking about?"

"He lied." Tears spring to my eyes. "Cole lied to the police. He lied to everyone. He wasn't driving the car when it crashed. I was."

She takes a step back. "What in the world makes you think that?"

"He told me." I wipe my eyes with the back of my hand. "I mean, he didn't say the exact words, but I'd been wondering ever since I saw the photo of me holding Dad's keychain, and he confirmed it. I was driving."

"Holy shit." Nathan takes off his hat and drags a hand through his hair. His shoulders slump. He walks a few paces away, shaking his head.

Vanessa meets my gaze, as if she's begging me to retract what I just said.

I steel my spine. "I was driving the car, Vanessa."

Anger flares over her face, the strike of a lightning bolt. "Bullshit."

"It's the truth."

"Cole told you that?" She fists her hands. "And you believed him? Are you fucking kidding me?"

My heartbeat kicks up. "No. I—"

"You let yourself get snowed by him is what you did." She backs up, her body vibrating with tension. "That's what you get for not listening to what the whole goddamned town had to say about Cole Danforth. He uses people, Josie. He fucks them over. That's exactly what he's doing to you."

"No, he's not."

Nathan hurries to Vanessa's side and puts his hand on her shoulder. "Maybe we should listen—"

"There's nothing to listen to!" She pushes his hand away, her tone bitter. "He's blaming her so he can clear his name before his stupid investors or the press find out the real truth." Spinning to face me, she spreads her arms out. "Don't you think it's a little coincidental that he told you this right when he's all over the news with Invicta's new whiskey brand?"

An ache constricts my chest, making it hard to breathe. "He didn't tell me anything. I figured it out."

"Because he's been working you this whole time," she retorts. "Planting ideas in your head because he knows you're vulnerable. Look at the facts, Josie. Don't you think the police would have figured it out if he'd been lying? And he totally caved with the lawsuit...paying it off without the smallest protest. It was a complete admission of guilt. *Everyone* knows it!"

"Vanessa, try to calm down." Nathan holds up his hands. "The baby…"

"The baby is fine," she snaps, swerving her gaze to him. "We both warned her about Cole when she first got here. I know he's an asshole, but to be so cruel to her? Can you believe this?"

"Yes," Nathan says.

The entire world stops. A dull noise thumps in my ears. The sound of my heartbeat is deafening.

Vanessa stares at him. "What?"

"I *can* believe it." He turns to me and lifts his palms. "Josie, I… I'm sorry. That night…there were things I didn't understand. Not only what Danforth said, but his statement and the evidence. It didn't fit that he could have gotten you out of the passenger seat at the rate the car was getting submerged. And the driver's seat… it was pushed close to the wheel, but not from the impact. Like the driver needed to be closer to reach the pedal, which didn't make sense since Danforth is so tall. But now…you driving the car? It makes sense. Everything."

Faint relief swirls through my shattered heart. If Nathan believes me, other people will too.

But…

I force my gaze to my sister. She's staring at Nathan as if she's never seen him before.

"That…" She clutches her hands together. "That's not true."

"It is." He encompasses us both with a pleading look. "Josie, I'm so sorry."

"For…for what?"

"Not telling anyone. Ah, hell." He groans and drags a hand over his face. "It was my father's investigation, and he was such a hard-ass, never thought I was good enough…I could never bring myself to stand up to him, and that night…I was just a rookie, and with all that was going on…no way could I tell him there were discrepancies in the evidence, or that what Danforth said didn't make sense…"

"A few bits of so-called evidence and you suddenly believe Cole has been lying for ten years?" Vanessa's voice rises. "And you think your *veteran police chief* father wouldn't have figured it out? But that you did?"

Nathan's face crumples. "No, I didn't. But knowing Josie was driving…"

"She wasn't driving!" Panic flashes in her expression. "He was."

My chest aches. "Vanessa, I *remember* some of it."

"You *remember* what he told you to remember." She presses her fingers to her temples, her eyes bright. "For ten years, you can't remember the first thing about the accident, then a few weeks after coming back and starting up with Cole again, you suddenly remember driving the car only because that's what he told you? You're damned right Cole is lying. But he's not lying to everyone. He's lying to *you*. And you're going to believe him over everything we *know*, regardless of what a rookie police officer thought he saw or heard? No."

Shaking her head, she backs away from both of us. "Don't you dare do this to yourself, Josie. Don't do this to me. Cole Danforth always has been and always will be the person responsible for killing our family. And I mean what I said even more now. Either you stay the hell away from him or you stay away from me and my son."

She strides off, her pace quickening.

"Vanessa…" Nathan runs after her.

"You stay away from me too." She turns and skewers him with a glare. "You're not even close to being the man I thought you were."

He comes to a halt, his chest heaving and jaw tight.

"And *you*." Vanessa shifts her gaze to me, her eyes hardening to chips of ice. "I wish to God you'd never come back."

She stalks toward the pier, her back rigid and fists clenched.

This is where I lose my sister again.

I approach Nathan cautiously and put my hand on his arm.

"Give her some time." I force a reassuring note into my voice. "I'll try and talk to her again."

His mouth twists. "I don't think she'll be willing to *talk* anytime soon."

Neither do I. Vanessa does not let go of anger and bitterness quickly. If ever.

Nathan turns to face me, letting out a long breath. "Are you okay? I know you've been trying to figure it out, but this…I never expected it. What are you going to do?"

I stare at my sister's retreating figure. "There's only one thing I *can* do."

CHAPTER 10

Josie

After declining Nathan's offer of a ride, I walk to downtown Castille. Lantern Square bustles with the usual morning crowd. Forcing my gaze to the Snapdragon Inn, I look up at the fifth-floor window. Cole's tall, distinctive shadow is etched against the glass.

I go into the lobby, where the security guard waves me to the stairs without calling to announce my arrival. By the time I reach the office, Cole is already pulling the door open.

His eyes are dark and smudged, his cheekbones hollowed. Lines crease his face, and thick stubble coats his jaw. Everything inside me crumples like a piece of paper crushed in a fist.

He steps aside to let me into his office and closes the door. He skims his gaze over my face, his hands clenching.

"Josie, I—"

"No, don't say anything." I hold up my hands and drag air into my lungs. "I can't…I'm so angry that you lied, even the other day at the pub when I asked you about the keys. For ten years, you…"

My voice cracks.

"I know. I'm so fucking sorry." A helpless look rises to his eyes, and my heart constricts. Not once has he ever been *helpless.*

"Are you sorry you lied or sorry I found out the truth?"

His jaw clenches. "Both."

I grip my hands together. "Even if I could understand why you did it in that moment, how could you have kept such a lie for so long?"

"Because I didn't want you to *know.*" His throat works with a hard swallow. "I never wanted to tell you or anyone else the truth. The only thing that scared the shit out of me was that you'd remember. But the longer time passed, the less chance there was that would happen. I didn't think you'd ever come back to Castille, and I sure as hell never planned to see you again. I just…I wanted you to live the rest of your life. To try and be happy again."

Tearing my gaze from him, I stare at the window overlooking the square. I'd once thought the dark was a place where you could go insane. Now I know it's *here*, in this horrible disconnect between the lie I've believed, *lived*, for ten years and the truth.

"But what…what about you?" The question splinters in my mouth.

Cole blinks. "What about me?"

"You took the blame." Overwhelming guilt knifes through me. "You…for all of it. Everyone in this town believed you were at fault. You paid off my sister's lawsuit, lost your trust fund, were forced to work for your father…your entire life went off track. Because of *me.*"

"No!" He strides toward me and grabs my shoulders. "Don't you fucking dare think I wouldn't have gone through that if it hadn't been for you."

"But you *wouldn't* have." Tears burn my eyes and clog my

throat. "You suffered for taking the blame. You still are. While I was still able to do what I'd planned."

"And that was what *I* wanted." He flexes his fingers desperately on my shoulders. "For you to do what you'd always wanted."

"And didn't it occur to you that I'd want the same for you?" Fresh anger fills me, though I no longer know where it's directed —at him, at myself, at the whole goddamned universe for ripping us apart, tearing open old wounds, and still not allowing us to heal. "I still loved you, Cole! I still wanted you to live your life, and now I find out that every single dream you ever had died right along with my parents and Teddy. And it was my *fault*."

"It was *not* your fault." His mouth compresses. "It was an accident. You told me you've never blamed me for it, so you *cannot* start blaming yourself."

"That was before you lied! How can you have sacrificed your whole life for it? For *me*? Didn't you know I'd be crushed to find out what happened to you? Didn't you think I wouldn't *want* you to do that, especially since not for one goddamned second over the past ten years have I stopped loving you?"

Cole stares at me, breathing fast. My heart expands and contracts at the same time.

Our life flashes between us, saturated with all the good, the frustrations, the hope. Everything spins and tumbles, all the little things that made us who we were together—pancakes, oil paint, salt-encrusted work boots, arguments about the calendar, cotton candy on the pier, sugary breakfast cereal. Bright, youthful *love*.

The tension in the air suddenly breaks, like a balloon bursting. We lunge toward each other. He captures me in his arms, lifting me hard against his powerful chest. Our mouths collide in a firestorm of longing and despair. My dark, tangled emotions unravel.

Oh, God.

Despite this suffocating pain, or maybe because of it, my body responds to him like a match set to dry tinder. Hunger explodes through me, an intense craving for all that he and I were together, everything we were just finding again. He puts his hand on my lower back, fitting our bodies together, and sweeps his tongue into my mouth. He tastes like everything I love—cherry candy, sunlight, Cole.

I press my hands to his face, smoothing his coarse stubble against my palms. Our tongues dart together, seeking and exploring. He takes two steps, and my back comes up against the wall. I drag my lips over his jaw to his neck, pressing my face into the hot juncture between his neck and shoulder. Our hearts beat together, rapid like birds' wings. I breathe him in. *Cole.*

"I love you." His words are rough, guttural against my skin. "Josie, I just...I love you so much. Tell me what to do to fix this. I'll do anything."

Bring my parents and Teddy back.

A chill rattles down my spine. Tightening my arms around him, I lift my head. Our gazes collide, sharp and desperate.

"I hate what this has done to you." I press one hand to his pounding heart. "Even now...people still see me as the tragic victim and you as the ruthless CEO. But when people find out the truth, they'll finally know you aren't who they've made you out to be."

He stills. "What are you talking about?"

Apprehension prickles my neck. It's no small consolation that word of this will change people's view of Cole...but it will also change everything for me. I'll go from victim to...what? Killer? Murderer? That's what people said about Cole. No one cared that the police investigation had determined it was an accident.

"I'm talking about telling people the truth," I say.

Cole releases me and steps away, his eyes darkening with shock.

"Jesus Christ, Josie." He flexes his hands. "You can't *tell* anyone."

I stare at him. "What?"

"No one knows, right?" He drags his palm over his face, his mouth bracketing with tension.

"Vanessa and Nathan do. I told them this morning. Nathan has always suspected something wasn't right about your statement, and now he knows why."

He curses, low and sharp. "I'll talk to him. Tell him to keep it quiet."

"Cole." Tenderness suddenly softens my anger. "It's over. I'm not letting you keep taking the blame for something that wasn't your fault."

"I could give a shit what people think about me." He paces to the other side of the room. "I never have. They don't deserve or need to know anything else. They'll make up their own versions of the truth anyway, so why put yourself in the line of fire?"

"Because I *hate* what people have been saying about you." I clench my hands. "I hate that Vanessa sued you over something you didn't even do. I hate that you paid her off. I hate that you've driven yourself so hard to build a fortress around you, to prove that no one can touch you. And now I hate that I've been the tragic survivor when I was the one who caused the accident. How can you think I wouldn't tell people?"

"To what end?" He spreads his arms out. "You'll be bringing up things that should stay in the past. Is that what you want? You want both of us to live through it all over again?"

"No. I want us to stop living a lie!"

"Goddammit, Josie." His features twist with regret. "I fucked up. I shouldn't have lied. But there is no way in hell I could have told the truth either. If I had to go back and do it all over again, I'd say the exact same thing. I would have lost my mind if I'd had to tell the police that you—"

His voice breaks off, his mouth thinning.

"That I was driving." A sharp ache pushes between my eyes. I stare out the window. My gaze stops on the bright, colorful mural.

The mural.

The painting I'd created in honor of my parents. The art for my mother, the history of Castille for my father. It will be here for years, for the whole town, a constant reminder of them and of…me.

"I have to go." I start toward the door. "I need to talk to Allegra, to tell her—"

"No." Cole darts in front of me and puts his hands up in a plea. "Don't do this to yourself. Don't do this to *us*."

Us.

"How can you…" My chest hitches. "How can you think I could ever keep this a secret knowing what you endured? I didn't just lose three people that night. I lost you too. And I can't…I can't live with this anymore. I won't let *you* live with it."

"Josie, it was my choice, everything was my choice."

"What about *my* choice?" Fresh anger flares through me. "I never had a chance to choose anything because I didn't even know what really happened. I didn't know what I'd survived, what I'd been responsible for. I never would have come back if I'd known. And God knows I don't deserve to do something in honor of my parents anymore."

"Don't say that." Desperation lines his face. "And please don't do this. Whatever you think I went through…and I'd do it all again a hundred times over if it meant protecting you…will all be for *nothing* if you tell people."

"The *truth* is not nothing, Cole." I yank open the door. "In fact, it's all I have left."

"No. Josie!"

I rush down the stairs and back outside. A shaft of sunlight blinds me. Instinct tells me to keep running, to escape, but the unfinished mural blocks my way.

Coming to a halt, I struggle to pull in air.

"Josie, don't." Cole hurries up beside me, his breath hard, his body vibrating with tension.

"I'm done." Grief and exhaustion crush me. "I can't finish this. After what I did…"

"Josie." Grabbing me with one hand, he points at the mural. "That is just one of the reasons you came back—to do something good in the world, right? So don't tell me you don't *deserve* to paint it when it's not only *good*, it's one of the best things that's happened to this community. Like you're the best thing that ever happened to me. And we are getting through this together. *I love you.*"

My heart squeezes into a tight, aching ball. Our love didn't survive the accident. There is no possible way it can survive the searing truth.

"Goddamn you, Cole Danforth." Tears spill over, and I pull away from him. "Goddamn you for lying, for leaving me, for making me believe we actually had a second chance, and most of all for loving me the way no other man ever will again."

He steps closer, pain filling his blue eyes, his hands reaching for me.

A ghostly pale face, a man reaching for me, blood gushing from a cut on his forehead, brown hair ragged and soaked…terrorized, ice-blue eyes…

I stumble back. Dizziness washes over me, spinning the world into chaos. I grab a bucket of red paint and pry off the lid. Time slows to a crawl.

Tires screeching. Screams, thin as needles puncturing my eardrums. My mother. Teddy's tiger. Smoke. Rain. Blood.

No!

I fling the paint at the mural. Red splashes over the panoramic design, drenching the sea creatures, the people gathered on the Water's Edge pier, the bright lights of the carnival. Obliterating the happy scene with a mess of dripping, splattered paint.

My chest heaves. Sweat runs down my back. People stop and stare.

I drop the bucket and start to run.

"Josie!"

Knowing Cole will come after me, I head for the woods. Even now, over twenty years after I first encountered him there, I can lose him in the tangle of trees and brush.

I keep going, desperate suddenly to run and keep running until the wind pushes me up into the sky, and I disappear.

CHAPTER 11

Josie

W e were a family. We still are.

I have one person left, and I can't lose her again. I won't.

Coming to a stop in front of the house on Poppy Lane, I struggle to catch my breath. Red paint still stains my hands. It feels like a million years since I discovered the truth, and yet it's only been two days.

Clouds gather overhead. A light rain falls. The windows are dark, and Vanessa's car isn't in the driveway.

I let myself into the house. The light on the answering machine blinks. I push it and listen to a message from an OBGYN nurse telling Vanessa she has to reschedule the appointment she missed this afternoon.

Shit. Where did she go? And didn't she just have an appointment the other day?

Pressing my hands to my temples, I try to think. She probably can't drive far in her clunky old Dodge, but she could get to the train station and go...anywhere. And she could cut me off entirely.

No.

Determination stiffens my spine. I hurry back to the foyer. My gaze lands on the key rack beside the door—one of the few things from our father that Vanessa hadn't put in the basement. Each hook is labeled for the key's purpose—*house, car, spare, garage, cottage, cabin.*

Relief fills me. I know where she is.

After a quick stop at Watercolor Cottage for supplies and extra clothes, I catch a bus to the base of Eagle Mountain. A sign marks the entrance to the woodlands scattered with hiking trails and camping sites. Hitching my backpack over my shoulders, I start hiking up Spiral Pass, keeping my thumb out in the hopes of catching a ride.

The rain comes down harder, gray clouds mixing with the onset of twilight. To my gratitude, two college kids on their way to a camping trip drive me to the cabin my father called *Heavenly Daze.* They leave me off at the start of a narrow dirt road leading to the trailhead.

Taking the left trail, I walk toward the cabin. I have countless memories of hiking in these woods with my family. Mom would always find a spot to sit and draw, waving Dad, Teddy, Vanessa and I on ahead while she stayed to create.

En route, Teddy collected rocks, leaves, sticks, dead bugs... anything he could find. Vanessa sighed and complained that her feet hurt. Dad marched forward, a walking stick in his hand, pausing every now and then to point out something he thought was fascinating—the way the light shone through the trees, the shape of a flower, a bird's nest.

The rustic wood cabin with its smudged windows and stone chimney appears in a clearing of pine trees. Vanessa's car is parked to the side, and the rumble of the generator indicates she got the electricity working.

Knowing she might turn me away, I suppress my nervousness and knock on the door. She opens it slightly, peering at me over the chain lock. Her face is pale and pinched, her swollen eyes smudged with dark circles.

I tighten my grip on my backpack. "Please let me come in."

She hesitates. Her lips compress. "I have nothing to say to you."

"You don't have to say anything." I indicate my damp hair and raincoat. "But it's raining, and I really don't want to walk all the way back to Spiral Pass."

The crease between her eyebrows eases a little. She unlatches the door and pulls it open. Relief and nostalgia flood me the instant I step inside. The musty cabin is still filled with old, comfortable furniture, woven throw rugs, and a bookshelf stuffed with books. My father's old nature lithographs and photos adorn the walls.

"Wow." I set my things down and take a deep breath. "It's like a time capsule."

"I was surprised too, though I don't know why." Vanessa purses her lips and surveys the room. "No one's been here in years so it's not as if anything would have changed."

Rubbing my hands together, I eye her cautiously. "How are you doing?"

She shrugs. Her expression closes off.

"Do I smell coffee?" I ask.

"Decaf. You can have a cup, if you want." She sits on the sofa, drawing an old quilt around her legs.

Since I'm *somewhat* certain she won't throw me out into the rain, I pour two cups of coffee and set a mug on the table for her.

"There was a message on the answering machine that you

missed a doctor's appointment this afternoon." I retrieve a paper bag from my backpack. "Is everything okay?"

"Yes. It was just for more bloodwork."

I sit across from her on the sofa and hand her the bag.

"What is it?" she asks.

"Open it. They might be a little squished though."

She peers into the bag. A faint smile curves her mouth. "I totally forgot. Dad's doughnuts."

"From Gus's Bakery." I unfold two napkins and hand her one. "Remember Gus always used to give Dad an extra one?"

"A baker's dozen." Vanessa takes out two chocolate-glazed doughnuts and sets one on a napkin for me.

"I couldn't fit a whole dozen in my backpack, so we'll have to settle for two. Well, three. Gus insisted on giving me an extra one anyway."

I bite into the sugary treat. Though it's ridiculous to get emotional about a chocolate-glazed doughnut, bittersweet pleasure fills me.

Before coming up to the cabin, our father always made a stop at Gus's Bakery for doughnuts. A baker's dozen. He wouldn't let anyone even open the box until we arrived at the cabin, after which we'd indulge in the ritual selection of one doughnut apiece before settling in for the weekend.

I polish off the doughnut, glancing up. Vanessa is watching me, her eyes shuttered.

Dismay clouds my heart. "I am *so* sorry, Vanessa."

She averts her gaze, her features tense.

Silence stretches thin and brittle.

"God." A sigh breaks from her throat. She pinches the bridge of her nose. "What a fucking mess."

"That's one way of putting it."

"I don't care what Nathan said." Leaning forward, she puts her mug on the coffee table with a thunk. "If he really thought he saw or heard something that contradicted Cole's story, then why the hell didn't the investigators and the chief of police notice them too?"

"Maybe they did." I rub my aching chest. "But Chief Peterson was good friends with Kevin Danforth, and he'd never thought Cole was worth anything. Just the opposite, especially after Cole broke away from his father. I imagine it was all too easy for him to believe that Cole had been driving. Hell, it was probably what he wanted. He wouldn't have had a problem ignoring any evidence to the contrary."

She twists her mouth with disbelief, but a glimmer of understanding appears in her eyes.

"So…do you believe it now?" My heart pounds.

She stares at her belly, stroking the round bump. Her eyes glitter.

"I don't know," she finally says. "I mean, all these years, and the lawsuit…Jesus. What are people going to think about that? What if Cole demands the money back?"

"He won't. He'll tell you what he told me. He made the choice." I drag my fingers through my damp hair. "I'm so…I mean, the lie was one thing, but it ended up changing his whole life. Ruining it."

With a faint laugh, she shakes her head. "I hardly think owning one of the most successful liquor companies in the country has *ruined* his life."

"But it wasn't what he wanted to do." I take a sip of coffee, smothering another surge of regret. "He was supposed to have a career in marine sciences and ocean conservation."

"So you just said *he made a choice*, right? I mean, if it's true that he lied about driving, I wouldn't call him a victim of circumstances. He still could have pursued marine sciences after he left Castille. For whatever reason, he chose not to. None of the events after the accident happened *to* him. He made them happen, both because of his lie and as a result of it."

"Maybe that's part of why he was upset when I told him I

wanted to tell the truth." I run my finger over the rim of my mug. "I was taking it all out of his control."

"Control does seem to be an issue with him." She rolls her eyes slightly.

"But nothing changes the facts." I pull in a heavy breath. "I was driving the car. It was my fault. Mom, Dad, Teddy…they'd still be alive if I'd done something differently."

Vanessa is silent for a second before she grabs my arm, her fingers tight.

"Stop it." Her voice sharpens. "Even after Cole left, you refused to believe he was at fault. You kept saying he hadn't killed them, that it was an accident, that there was nothing he could have done. You defended him constantly. So don't you dare turn things around on yourself now. If you were the driver, you couldn't have done anything to stop it. No one will blame you."

"What about you?" I scrub my swollen eyes with my sleeve. "You blamed Cole, so why wouldn't you blame me? The circumstances were the same."

She compresses her lips. "I was furious after the accident… obviously. Grief-stricken. And ever since then, Cole has never done a thing to make people, me included, think anything *good* about him. It's like he wanted to live up to the rumors that he'd done something wrong. So yes, I blamed him for a lot of things. And now I know he *wanted* to be blamed. He lied. He put it on himself. And he did it for *you*."

Releasing my arm, she sits back and shakes her head again. "I guess it was pretty selfless. He wasn't thinking about himself at all. The only thing he cared about was protecting you from the worst nightmare you could have imagined." She spreads out her hand and looks at her fingers. "Most women would give a lot to be loved *that* much."

The statement lodges like a tiny light beneath my layers of sorrow and grief.

Vanessa sighs, her shoulders slumping. "And I'm sorry for

what I said. I hate what's happening, but it's okay that you came back. In fact, I'm glad you did."

"I am too. But I don't think I can finish the mural."

She frowns. "Why not?"

"An honor for Mom and Dad when I—"

My voice breaks off. Pain flashes in Vanessa's eyes.

"How can I finish it without thinking about what I did?" I rub a speck of dried red paint on my thumb.

"You can't."

"What?"

"You're not supposed to finish the mural without thinking of them." She reaches for her mug. "You're supposed to finish it *by* thinking of them. When you were six years old, you broke one of Mom's clay sculptures that was supposed to be in an art show in Portland."

I blink at the non-sequitur. "I don't remember that."

"I do. You were running around the house pretending to be Wonder Woman, sliding down the banister, using a rope as a lasso. And on one of your rescue missions or whatever, you bumped into the table that was holding the sculpture. It fell and broke into about half a dozen pieces. Totally ruined."

"How horrible." I search for the memory but can't find it. "Mom must have been horrified."

"She was. She didn't have another piece to send them, and she didn't have time to make one so she had to drop out of the show."

"Yeah, this isn't making me feel better at all."

Vanessa smiles faintly. "My point is that she didn't blame you. She didn't even scold you for running in the house because, of course, we used to do that all the time. She just said it was an accident and that there would be another art show. You helped her pick up the pieces and moved on. I guarantee she would want you to do the same thing now."

My heart constricts. "Breaking a sculpture and causing a fatal car crash are two different things entirely."

"My point is that they were both accidents." An urgent note threads Vanessa's voice. "And Mom and Dad never blamed you for an accident. God knows we had a lot of them as kids. The sculpture was just one of many. And yes, I know this is different, but if you think they'd blame you, you would be wrong."

Something loosens inside me, like a tight, frayed knot starting to unravel. I reach for the last doughnut in the bag and split it apart. We both polish off half before Vanessa groans and pushes to her feet.

"I need to get some sleep." She runs a hand over her belly. "The baby's been kicking all day, and he's finally settled down so this is my chance."

"I hope all that sugar doesn't get him going again." I take our mugs to the sink. "Do you need me to make up the bed?"

"No, I already did it. I brought some sheets."

"I'll sleep on the sofa." I walk to where she's standing outside the bedroom door. "Why did you come up here anyway?"

"Just to get away." She sighs and gathers her hair away from her neck. "I knew you and Nathan would come to the house looking for me, and...I needed to think. If it's really true, then I feel like shit for the way I treated Cole. What I did to him."

"But you didn't know, Vanessa. None of us knew." I spread my hands out. "When information is kept from us, all we have to contend with is what we *think* we know. And I have no idea what's going to happen with me and Cole, but I do know I can't lose *you* again too. I came back to Castille for you and for the baby. We need each other."

She ducks her head. Tears shine in her eyes. She steps toward me for a quick embrace, which somehow says more than words could.

"Get some sleep, Josie." She detaches herself from me and turns to the bedroom. "You look like you could use it."

For the first time in what seems like ages, I laugh.

CHAPTER 12

Josie

"Josie? Josie!"

I startle, opening my eyes. Lights blaze through the cabin. Vanessa is standing beside the sofa, shaking my arm. Her hair falls on either side of her face, shadowing her expression.

"What?" I sit up groggily. "Are you okay?"

"I don't know." She presses a hand to her belly.

I blink, my sleepiness turning into alarm. "What's wrong?"

"I've had a few contractions." She sits beside me, her forehead creased. "I didn't think much of it at first, but the last one was kind of strong."

"But you're not due for over a month."

"That's why it's weird." She shifts and winces, still rubbing her belly. "It's probably just false labor, but…I don't know."

"Let's call your doctor." I rummage in my backpack for my phone and swipe the screen. "Shit. No signal."

"We never got a signal up here." She makes a *tsk* noise and shakes her head. "That's why Dad liked it so much—because it cut us off from technology for a few days. I think that might have been one of the reasons he bought this particular cabin."

"I guess he never thought a situation might arise where we'd need to call someone." I toss the phone aside, concern prickling my skin. "What are we supposed to do? Time them or something?"

"I don't think so." She leans her head against the back of the sofa. "I mean, I can't be in labor."

She doesn't sound sure about that, and her uncertainty strengthens my concern. For something to do, I push to my feet and get her a bottle of water from the fridge.

"Let's time them just to see if there's a pattern." I open the water and hand it to her before pulling up the stopwatch on my cell. "Tell me when one starts."

For the next hour, we time her contractions, which last less than twenty seconds and are a good fifteen minutes apart.

"That's not very much." She reaches behind her to rub her lower back. "But I'm a little freaked out that they're not stopping completely. Braxton-Hicks contractions aren't supposed to get longer."

I glance at the list I've made on a notepad recording the time of each contraction. The first one we timed was twelve seconds. The last one was eighteen.

Don't panic. At least, don't let her know you're panicking.

"Maybe we should head back to town," I suggest, managing to keep my voice calm. "Sooner rather than later."

She nods and hauls herself to her feet. "Let me get dressed and go to the bathroom."

After pulling on jeans and a T-shirt, I hurry to throw a few things into my backpack. I grab my most powerful flashlight and get Vanessa's travel bag and car keys from the bedroom.

Only when I open the front door to take our bags to the car

do I realize it's still raining. Hard. Water streams from the gutters and puddles in the bumpy dirt road, and a heavy wind rustles the pine trees.

A lump sticks in my throat. Swallowing it back down, I shrug into my bright red raincoat, flip on the light, and dash through the rain to toss my backpack in the trunk.

Not wanting to think about *driving in the goddamned rain*, I run back inside to help Vanessa to the car.

I skid to a halt. She's standing outside the bathroom, pale with shock and holding a...

"Vanessa." Ice slithers through my veins. "What is that?"

"Blood." She stares at the bloody tissue, then looks back at me. "I'm bleeding. I shouldn't be bleeding like this."

Jesus.

My stomach knots. Grabbing the tissue from her, I throw it in the trash.

"Come on." I take her arm. She's shaking so hard her teeth chatter. "I put our stuff in the car. We'll be at the hospital in no time."

Hurrying through the rain, we manage to get back out to the car. I help her get situated in the backseat and run back to the cabin for a pillow so she can lie down on her side. Then I get into the driver's seat.

My heart is pounding so hard it's like thunder in my head. I push the key into the ignition, struggling to keep my breathing even.

I can do this. *I have to do this.*

After starting the windshield wipers, I push the gear shift into drive and head toward Spiral Pass. My sweaty palms slip on the wheel. The tires bump.

I glance in the rearview mirror at Vanessa. In the dim light, her eyes are closed, her head resting on the pillow. One hand is on her belly.

Get a grip, Josie Mays. This is not about you.

I pull carefully on to Spiral Pass, hoping my internal scolding is enough to quell my growing panic. There are no other cars on the road, which at first I think might be a relief. But as I press on the accelerator and pick up speed, my nerves stretch tighter and tighter.

Dark rainy night...only car on the road...

Blocking the thought, I flex my fingers on the wheel and concentrate on the mechanics of driving. The headlights carve a dim path through the rain, illuminating only the yellow dividing line and the wet asphalt ahead. Beyond that thin light, there is only vast, suffocating dark.

I drag in a deep breath and let it out slowly.

"You doing okay?" Not taking my eyes off the road, I force a light note into my voice.

Vanessa doesn't respond. I can't risk looking at her. I tighten my grip on the wheel and press the accelerator a little harder. Though I'm well below the speed limit, the *whoosh* of the tires in the water makes the car feel as if it's going way too fast. Ahead looms the sharpest curve on the mountain.

I brake on a shallow turn. My chest tightens. The hill slopes down on either side of the narrow road, plunging into nothing but darkness.

"Ellsworth is out with a knee injury, but Walker is batting a .300."

"The Dodgers should never have traded him."

"Hey, if we go early we should try one of the new restaurants at Fenway."

Cole's and my father's voices drift through the car, a harmony to the sound of the rain pummeling the roof and windshield. I'm happy and tired from the success of the party, but my hands clench tighter on the wheel the harder the rain falls.

I should have let Cole drive. He navigates storms better than I do. Maybe I should pull over and...

No, it's okay. We'll be home in fifteen minutes. If I stop, we might

wake Teddy up. There's the sign for the Old Mill Bridge. Once we cross
that, it's just a few more turns back into Castille.

I flip the wipers to a faster speed as we approach the bridge. The
streets in town must be flooding with all this rain. I can't see anything
past the gleam of the headlights.

Braking, I navigate the car over the bridge, then accelerate slightly
as we pull away from it. Water pours from the road down the slope
leading to the rocky ocean shore.

I need to brake on this turn...Dad always reminds me it's a sharp
one, and you never know if—

Oh my God. Brake! I can't see. What just...oh, shit, the wheel...we're
in a spin...the tires...Cole's hand, his voice...is that a scream? What the
hell is...oh no....no...NO!

Dark.

I slam on the brakes. My blood is ice, my breath shallow. I rest
my head on the steering wheel and drag air into my tight lungs.

"Josie." Vanessa's strained plea prickles my skin.

I squeeze my eyes shut. Shame chokes my throat.

Goddammit. Stop being a coward, Josie. Drive the damned car!

I grip the wheel again, determination steeling my spine. My
fear will not win.

"It's okay, sorry." I press the accelerator, guiding the car
forward. "Just thought I saw something in the road."

I keep driving. Foot on the brake. Hands controlling the
wheel. Brake. Turn. Steady. I can do this. I *am* doing this.

A strange calm settles over me. The dark isn't scary. Not
anymore. What's fucking scary is *living* in the dark when you
know there's so much light out there. When you won't let yourself open the doors to find it.

"Remember Dad's songs?" I flex my fingers on the wheel. "He
used to make us sing the whole way up the mountain. 'Oh My
Darling Clementine' was his favorite."

"God." Vanessa chokes out a laugh. "The most morbid folksong in history. The girl with gigantic feet gets a splinter and dies. Lovely."

I chuckle. "Teddy's favorite was 'Big Rock Candy Mountain.' Lemonade springs where the bluebird sings. He thought the—"

The car jolts, tires skidding. My heart stutters. *What the...*

"What was that?" Panic threads Vanessa's voice.

A popping noise comes from the engine. Clutching the wheel, I press the brake slowly. *God in heaven, please don't let the brakes fail.*

The pedal catches under the pressure of my foot, slowing the car. My pulse thunders in my head. The engine rattles and churns. I manage to get the car to the side of the road and pull to a stop.

"What's happening?" Vanessa asks.

"I'm not sure. Hold on." I shove the gearshift into drive and try the accelerator.

The car lurches forward and stalls. *No. Please, no.*

I turn off the ignition and restart the car. After a rumbling turnover, the engine sputters and dies.

No fucking way.

Hitting the hazard lights, I check the gas gauge. Three-quarters of a tank. I pump the accelerator a few times, press the brake, and turn the key. The engine cranks again and dies.

I grab my cell and swipe the screen. Plenty of battery, but no signal.

Wait a second. There's a narrow road just off Spiral Pass leading to an old stone tower. Vanessa once told me it's one of the few spots on the mountain that has a clear cell signal.

If I can make it there, I can call 911. I have no idea how long it will take for an emergency vehicle to reach us, but at least someone will know we're in trouble.

Where is the tower? Have I passed it or is it just around the next turn?

"Josie, what's going on?"

"Just a stall." I turn to look at my sister, trying to keep my expression calm. "I'm going to try and get a cell signal. Don't get out of the car. I'll be right back."

Before she can ask another question, I tuck my phone underneath my raincoat, grab the flashlight, and get out of the car. I'll go a short distance and see if I can find the path.

Shining the light ahead of me, I hurry along the side of the road. Rain pours down. My shoes slip on wet gravel and leaves. I try not to think about the steep drop to my right.

The path to the tower is just ahead...maybe one more turn...

Two headlights burn through the wet darkness ahead of me. A car ascending the mountain.

Relieved panic tightens my chest. *What if they don't see us? What if they don't stop?*

I pivot and rush back to the car, waving my flashlight and trying to keep my red raincoat in the beam in the hopes of catching the driver's attention. I'm halfway back when the car crosses the line and pulls over, tires skidding on the gravel.

"Josie!" A familiar deep voice cuts through the darkness like a stream of gold.

Cole. Holy shit.

Every part of me collapses and opens at the same time. Relief surges like a blue sea-wave underneath my heart.

Spinning on my heel, I run toward him. He catches me, closing his strong hands around my arms. In the beam of the flashlight, his expression is shadowed with concern and fear.

"It's Vanessa." Grabbing his hand, I haul him toward the Dodge. "She's...the baby's in trouble. The car broke down. I was trying to get to the stone tower to see if I could get a cell signal."

"It's a good three miles back." He runs toward the car and yanks open the door.

I open the other door, shining the flashlight on my sister.

She's even paler than before, her breathing shallow, both hands gripping her belly. A dark stain spreads between her legs over her gray sweatpants.

"Vanessa." Cole puts his hand on the side of her head, forcing her to look at him. "I'm going to bring my car closer, then we'll help you get into the backseat, okay? Josie, stay with her."

He dashes back into the rain. I grip my sister's hand. Our eyes meet. Hers are black with panic.

"I can't lose this baby," she whispers.

"You won't." I tighten my grip on her hand. "I swear, Vanessa. You won't."

Conviction steels my spine. Cole pulls his car up beside ours, and we get Vanessa transferred into the backseat. Grabbing my backpack, I climb into the passenger seat. Cole eases back onto the road, his profile rigid.

"Keep your cell out," he orders. "When you get a signal, call the Fernsdown Hospital and tell them we're on the way. It's the closest from here."

"What…why were you coming up Spiral Pass?" My teeth start to chatter.

"I went to the cottage to see if you were okay." He tightens his grip on the wheel, his knuckles burning white. "Some of your stuff was gone, and you weren't at the house either. This was the only other place I could think of where you would have gone. I wasn't going to bother you, I was *trying* not to, but when it got dark and rainy, I—"

His voice breaks off abruptly.

The *opening* sensation beneath my fear expands a little more. He'd been worried I wouldn't have enough lights, that I'd get scared and panic like I did that first night at the cottage. He needed to make sure I was safe.

Just like he always has before.

The sports car hugs the curves and makes turns in the road

with ease. Spiral Pass widens as we reach the base of the mountain. When the road intersects with Highway 19 running from Castille to Fernsdown, the blurry headlights of other cars appear through the darkness.

"I've got a signal." I swipe the screen of my phone and bring up the hospital number.

"Tell them we'll be there in five minutes."

After a few more turns, the lights of the hospital appear. Relief floods me. Cole pulls up in front of the emergency room entrance, and I scramble out to find help.

By the time two medics arrive with a wheeled stretcher, Cole is already helping Vanessa out of the backseat. She's still pale, her forehead dotted with sweat and her eyes glazed. The medics point me to the desk where I need to fill out the paperwork before they sweep Vanessa through to the emergency room.

My breath scorches my lungs, and my heart is racing. Rain puddles at my feet. A prickling sensation skates down my spine.

I turn. Cole is standing behind me, his raincoat open, his hair drenched, and his unerring gaze fixed on me.

"Go with her." He puts his hand on my lower back, urging me toward the double doors. "They'll give you a change of clothes too. I'll deal with the car and the paperwork."

There are a hundred things I want to say to him, but I can't shape any of them into a coherent sentence. Instead I grab him around the waist and squeeze, my heart hammering and gratitude choking my throat.

He closes his arms around me. I bury my face in his damp shirtfront. His heart beats heavily, thumping into my blood.

"I love you." He presses his lips to the top of my head. "I never stopped loving you, Josie Bird. You are my hero."

Tears sting my eyes. There are still so many unanswered questions, uncertainties, things we don't know.

But isn't that all...*life*?

Cole eases away from me and takes a wad of tissues from his raincoat pocket.

I manage to smile. "Do they have lotion?"

"What do you think?" He runs his hand over my hair and nods toward the emergency room doors.

Wiping my eyes, I turn and rush after my sister.

CHAPTER 13

Cole

I run past the Water's Edge pier, over the path through the park, and down to the harbor. Blood pumps through my veins. My muscles ache from strain, but it's a good feeling. Breathing fast, lungs working, heart pounding. Being alive.

The rising sun throws a reddish-gold glow on the water. Fishermen and workers crowd the docks, getting their gear and boats ready for the day. I slow to a walk and catch my breath.

At the other end of the cove is the boathouse where I rented a room in college. How many times did I wake before dawn, pulling on bib pants and boots before heading out for hours on a lobster boat? Hauling traps in the blazing sun. Washing down the deck. Counting the catch.

"You just going to stand there or get to work?" A grizzled old salt peers at me from beside a pile of traps.

"Can't work any better than you, Pete."

With a grunt, he lifts a trap from the stack. "Yeah, well, you get sick of bartending, you come back and do some real work."

"I'll think about it."

"Pussies *think*. Men *do*."

Grinning, I start back across the docks. After a run to the end of the pier, I head downtown. Josie has texted me several times since yesterday, assuring me that everything has gone well with Vanessa. Her son was born shortly after we got to the hospital, and though preterm, he's healthy and doing well. Since I don't know if Vanessa will want me to visit, I've kept my distance.

I reach Lantern Square and cross the street. Nathan Peterson is approaching a coffee-house from his parked police car. We both stop.

"Danforth." He takes off his sunglasses. His forehead creases. "I heard what happened. Glad everyone is okay."

"So am I."

"I also..." He twists his mouth and glances past me. "That night...I didn't do the job I should have. I owe you an apology."

"You don't owe me anything. You..." I clear my throat. "You stayed with Josie. Thank you."

He shrugs and meets my gaze. I get why he never told his father about his suspicions. I know a lot about difficult fathers.

"Have a good day," he finally says.

"Yeah. You too."

I walk to the Snapdragon Inn, intending to shower and change in my office bathroom before driving out to Spring Hills. Someone cleared Josie's paint and supplies away from the garden wall, but the mural itself remains untouched. The pier, carnival, and a good portion of the ocean are still obliterated by splatters of red paint.

My chest tightens. I open the lobby door and stop. Allegra King is standing by the security desk, tapping one foot impatiently. The guard gives me an apologetic shrug.

"Cole." Allegra nods sharply. "I'd like to speak with you, please."

Though I'm in no mood for a confrontation, I've never backed down from Allegra's ire. Gesturing for her to precede me on the stairs, we walk to my office.

"This must be a big deal, if you've come all the way over here." I toss my keys on the desk and cross my arms.

"It is." She steps toward me, hands on her hips and a hard glint in her eyes. "It's been brought to my attention that you've been lying to us."

I clench my jaw. "Has it?"

"Yes. You've been lying for quite some time to the entire town."

"That shouldn't surprise anyone."

"Actually, it does." She lifts her eyebrows. "It shocks the hell out of me, to be frank."

"Why?" I flex my hands against my biceps. "Because you should have figured it out sooner?"

"Maybe." She purses her lips, studying me. "Though you've never been an easy one to figure out, you've also never given me much reason to like you. Not that I do now," she adds hastily.

A reluctant smile tugs at my mouth. "I'd never expect such an honor."

"It does take effort to rise in my personal esteem," she says. "But I will admit that you might have moved up a notch given what has just come to light."

I'm not sure what to make of that remark. "I will never feel the need to explain this to anyone, but I lied for one reason only. Josie Mays. If anyone has a problem with that, they take it up with me. Not her."

Faint amusement creases her eyes at my echo of her statement to me back when Josie first arrived in Castille.

"That's not what I'm talking about," she says. "Though I do find what you did quite...fearless. Most people seem to agree with me, even if lying to the police and giving a false statement are against the law."

My shoulders tense. "I didn't do it to be fearless or break the law. *She* was my only reason."

"I know. And I've already discussed this with the chief of police, who has no intention of reopening the case or filing any charges." She narrows her eyes and taps her fingers against her hips. "However, I've discovered that this isn't the only secret you've been keeping."

"What does that mean?"

"When were you planning to tell me about the toxin you found in half a dozen springs that supply drinking water from Castille to Fernsdown?" Allegra asks. "Something called *perchlorate*?"

Averting my gaze, I scratch the back of my neck. "I have no idea what you're talking about."

"Odd since it's part of a story I just read about you on a website called *Drink Me*. The reporter claims that you've hired scientists and a contaminant removal team to purify the springs and that you've started testing more water sources in the area. At considerable personal expense."

My insides twist. The reporter Billy Grant didn't get that information out of nowhere.

"I'm building a distillery out by Spring Hills and scouting another location." I meet her gaze again. "I won't build near a tainted water source, so it makes business sense to purify the springs. I'm not a hero, Allegra."

"I know." She brushes a hand over her perfectly styled hair. "Lucky for you, I don't particularly care for heroes. They can be a bit self-righteous, don't you think?"

A sudden laugh rumbles out of me. This is the weirdest conversation she and I have ever had.

"I might have misjudged you, Mr. Danforth." Allegra picks up her purse and strides to the door. "I'm not convinced yet, but it's an idea I'm considering. However, that doesn't mean I like you."

"Too bad. Because I think I'm starting to like you."

Her lips twitch, falling short of an actual smile. She throws me a pointed look and leaves the room.

I turn on my computer and bring up the *Drink Me* website. Billy Grant's interview with me is on the first page, peppered with photos of the Invicta distilleries and products. Toward the end of the interview are the details about our work with contaminant removal and research teams to purify the area water.

After grabbing my phone, I hit a number from my contacts list. My uncle Gerald answers.

"What did you tell that reporter?" I snap.

"The facts. You should finally be familiar with them."

"You're fired."

"Nope." He chuckles. "You're no Boy Scout, Cole. But believe it or not, sometimes you make business decisions that actually help other people. Maybe it's an unintended consequence. Maybe not. But I guarantee you'll sleep better at night when you admit that's the truth."

Ending the call, I look out the window at the mural. Despite the splatter of red, the panorama of the town's history gleams bright and vibrant in the afternoon sunlight.

I retrieve my keys and head downstairs to my car. After stopping at a supply store, I return to the mural. All of the secrets Josie included are tucked away like little treasures—the figures of her parents and Teddy, the two of us on the Ocean Carousel, the man standing on Eagle Cliff.

I open a few tubes of paint, take out a brush, and add my own secret to the wall.

CHAPTER 14

Josie

The day after our frantic drive down the mountain, I wake with a strange feeling. It's like something weighing me down has lifted, allowing oxygen to circulate through my blood.

Bright light streams through the cottage window. The sun is high, almost as if it's—

Rolling over, I peer at the clock. Ten a.m. I've been asleep for seven hours. I didn't have a single dream that I can recall. I certainly didn't have any nightmares. It was a good sleep, heavy and unbroken, the kind that repairs and restores.

About time, Mr. Sandman.

I hurry to dress so I can get to the hospital to visit Vanessa. When I arrive, she's sitting up in bed with her newborn son in her arms. Though the birth wasn't easy and the baby will be spending the next few days in the NICU, all of his vital stats and tests are well within proper range.

"Did you decide on a name?" I gather the baby in my arms, unable to take my eyes off his scrunched-up face.

"What do you think of Benjamin Theodore?"

I lift my gaze to hers. A wave of warmth and sorrow passes between us.

"Benjamin Theodore." I nuzzle the baby's little head. My throat constricts. "I love it."

"Me too." Vanessa reaches out to touch her son's hand. "And thanks for being there for me. I'm really glad you were."

I sit beside the bed and adjust the baby in my arms. I plan to still be there for her. For both of them.

"I wonder if there's a collective noun for babies in that book you told me about." Vanessa settles back against the pillows. "Like a *pod* of babies."

"A cuddle of babies," I suggest.

"Ah, good one."

I stay for another hour, reluctantly handing Benjamin back when I remember all the things I still have to do.

"I should get going. I have unfinished business to finish, one of which is painting Benjamin's nursery."

"What about the town mural?" Vanessa slants me a glance.

Anxiety ripples down my spine. The Bicentennial Festival is in one week. And not only did I abandon the mural, I vandalized it. I don't know what the festival committee and Allegra King will say about it, but I'm not going to run away again.

Before I can respond to my sister's question, a light knock sounds at the door. Nathan peers inside, clad in his police officer uniform and holding a bouquet of flowers and a gift bag.

"Okay if I come in?" He looks uncertainly at Vanessa.

"Yes." Her expression softens. "How did you know I was here?"

"A little bird told me." He winks at me in silent thanks.

Vanessa gives me a mock glower, but she can't conceal the pleasure in her eyes.

Nathan peers at the baby. "Wow, look at him. He's perfect."

"Do you want to hold him?"

"Uh, sure. I think so."

She shifts Benjamin from her arms into Nathan's. He looks down at the little bundle with an expression of such awe that my heart lightens. Whatever happens between him and Vanessa, he's demonstrated not only his strength and decency as a man, but his loyalty as well.

"I'm going to go." I squeeze my sister's leg by way of a goodbye.

"Okay." She hesitates. "Have you seen Cole?"

"Not since yesterday." I rub my hands on my jeans. "I'm going to stop by his office now."

Though a shadow clouds her eyes, she nods. "Tell him thank you from me."

"I will." Pleased by the small overture, I give Benjamin one last pat. "I'll call you later."

Leaving her and Nathan alone with the baby, I walk out to the car I've rented for the next few days. I haven't conquered my fear of driving in one fell swoop, but at least now I'm facing it head-on.

After returning to Lantern Square, I hurry toward the Snap-dragon Inn. A glimpse of the red-splattered mural constricts my heart, but I have to deal with that later.

Cole is waiting for me in his office, and the sight of him—in a tailored suit and tie, his golden-brown hair falling over his fore-head—eases whatever tension I have left. Something appears to have loosened inside him too, smoothed his frown lines, maybe even softened him a little.

He greets me with a smile and extends his arms. Relieved, I fit myself against him and press my head to his chest. His heart thumps strong and steady into my ear, timeless as ever.

"You okay?" He presses a kiss to the top of my head.

"I think so." I tighten my arms around his waist. "Starting to be okay, at least. You?"

"I'm good."

I ease back to look at him. "Even though people are finding out that…"

"Josie." He rests his hand on my neck, the lines of his forehead relaxing. "Whatever happens, I want us to deal with it together. And it sounds like what will always be painfully immediate for us is a tragic but distant part of the past for most other people. It's time for all of us to start looking forward."

I press my palm against his heart. "Vanessa asked me to thank you."

"She and the baby are doing well?"

"Yes. I don't think it'll be too long before you're able to meet Benjamin Theodore."

"Great name." His eyes crinkle with warm tenderness. "Let me know when it'll be okay to send him a gift. Stuffed animal, pacifier, college fund…"

I grin. "I'll keep you posted."

"I need to go to New York for a few days, but I'll be back in time for the festival." He slides his hand to my nape. "Hopefully before."

I lift an eyebrow. "You're going to the festival?"

"Invicta is sponsoring it, so I guess I have to." He shrugs. "I'm hoping they need another judge for the pie bake-off."

Tycoon Cole judging a pie bake-off. Might be one for the papers. "If you're judging, I might have to bake a cherry pie."

He frowns. "Okay, but I won't play favorites. Oh, hell, yes I will. But only for you."

"Hmm. Maybe I'll have to reward you with your own special cherry pie."

"I am a big fan of your cherries."

With a laugh, I stand on tiptoe to press my lips to his. We

indulge in a lengthy kiss before he lifts his head and threads his hand through my hair.

"See you in a week?" he asks.

"I'll be waiting for you." I smile and look into his eyes. And right there in the blue, gold-flecked depths is the boy who saved my Halloween candy and the man who saved me.

After Cole leaves for his trip, I work on finishing the baby's nursery. Vanessa and Benjamin are released from the hospital, and I help them both get settled at home before I return to the mural.

Everything is exactly as I'd left it. I'd sent Allegra King a text that I'd be back, though I'm prepared to work on the painting alone since word of my meltdown and everything surrounding it has traveled. There's no way I can finish the mural in time for the festival, but I'll work as hard as I can.

I set up the paints, drop cloths, and brushes. My hand shakes a little as I start to cover up the red splatters and repaint the pier and carnival, but the bright, twinkling lights and neon signs quickly shine through.

"Do you need some help?"

I glance up. Charlotte is standing nearby, her brown hair pulled into a ponytail. She smiles and gestures to her worn jeans and old T-shirt.

"I dressed for the job," she adds.

"I would love some help." Gratitude swells, and I reach for a clean brush. "Thanks so much. Hey, I have something for you."

After giving her the brush, I dig into my backpack for the evil-eye amulet and extend it to her. "I so appreciate this, but I don't need it anymore."

"You sure?" Lifting an eyebrow, she slips the amulet into her pocket.

"I'm sure." *I already have all the protection I need.*

She gets started painting a colonial-era building, and I return to covering up the red splatters.

"Can I help?"

It's David, one of my father's old friends from the Historical Society. As the morning progresses, more and more people stop to paint—some for just a few minutes, and others for an hour or more. Allegra King even shows up, though the sight of her prickles me with nervousness.

"First, congratulations on the birth of your new nephew," she tells me. "I'm glad everything worked out so well."

"So am I. Thank you." I grip my paintbrush tighter. "I wanted to apologize for what happened with the mural. I wasn't in a very—"

Allegra's raised hand stops my words. "Josie, there is no need to apologize. I can't even imagine how difficult it's been for you. I certainly don't hold you accountable, and I don't believe anyone else will either. This community has always supported you, and you'll find that we will continue to do so. Now more than ever."

"Thank you." Relieved, I gather my courage for my next statement. "Also, I was hoping to talk to you more about the Arts Center. You'd mentioned you'd like me to be on the recruitment committee when you start hiring new teachers and artists."

"Yes, and the offer still stands," she replies. "If you already have some names for us, that would be lovely."

"I have one name." I take a deep breath. "Josie Mays."

Surprise widens her eyes. "Really? But I thought you were going home soon."

"I need to go to Los Angeles after the festival for an exhibition opening," I explain. "But I've been thinking about what Eve said about community-based art. The mural has helped me realize how important it is. There's so much that can be accomplished with youth education, outreach to disenfranchised communities, more collaborative efforts with installations. I'll do some research and can write up a proposal and send you my resume with—"

"Josie." With a laugh, Allegra holds up her hand again. "Say no more. We would love to have you as part of the Arts Center staff."

I blink. "Really?"

"Of course. Not only are you a talented artist, you also have a talent for involving people in art. And the fact that you have strong ties to this community...well, you're the ideal person for the job."

"Thank you *so* much." I can't help giving her a quick hug of gratitude. "I'd also like to talk to you about another concrete wall that could use some beautification over by the pier."

"Come to my office tomorrow, and we'll discuss it further." She squeezes my hands warmly. "Welcome home, Josie. Now what can I paint?"

After I give her several brushes, she gets started painting the flags on Lantern Street.

As I return to my task repainting the pier, a dot of red in the center of the woods catches my eye. Another paint splatter. I dip a brush into the sage-green paint and peer more closely at the clusters of trees and branches stretching out past the lighthouse.

My heart leaps. Marching along a trail is a little girl wearing shorts and a Scooby-Doo T-shirt. Her dark hair is pulled into a ponytail, and she's carrying a red backpack decorated with big yellow daisies. A scarlet red tanager flies at her side.

That girl is right at home in the woods, in this town where her mother created colorful, expansive images of mystical women, where her father delivered the mail and traced the lineage of Castille schooners, where her sister taught her how to put on lipstick, where her little brother played with Legos and learned how to pitch a baseball, and where she'd grow up to fall in love with the boy she had a crush on when she was nine.

A smile opens up from the middle of my soul, and a strange

feeling lifts my heart. For an instant, I don't recognize it. It's light and airy, almost sparkly, like a purple balloon rising into the sky.

Happiness.

&

As late afternoon approaches, I drive out of Castille toward the lighthouse and turn off on to a coastal road bordered by grasslands. On a hill above the ocean, an old stone church presides over a cemetery dating back two centuries.

I park at the entrance and walk past the headstones to a grove of trees. Sheltered under the branches is a small grave set between two larger ones.

When Teddy was little, he used to love walking between our parents, holding their hands so they could lift him and swing him back and forth. Being boosted off the ground and flown through the air never failed to make him laugh with joy. And though at twelve he was too big for hand-swinging, he never lost the habit of walking between Mom and Dad.

Kneeling, I place my hand on my little brother's grave. Maybe now, wherever they all are, it doesn't matter how big or old Teddy is. Maybe they're all in a place where he can still grab Mom and Dad's hands and swing as much as he wants.

Maybe that's what happens after we leave this life—we go to a place where we're with the people we love, and we can do whatever makes us the happiest. Whatever makes us laugh with joy.

A breeze rustles through the trees. Birds chirp. I sit for a long time, grateful for what I've been given and hoping to find my way into the peace I know my parents want for me.

I love you, Mom.

I love you, Dad.

I love you, Teddy.

Getting to my feet, I pick up my red backpack and hitch it over my shoulder. As I return to the path, I stop.

A raven, glossy feathers black as ink, stands near a tree. He rustles his wings in the breeze and turns his head. His black eyes fix on mine. An eternity passes in those few seconds.

The raven hops forward on both feet, then shifts to a walk beyond the trees. Pushing his head forward, he caws, throat feathers ruffling. His wings open and start to flap, lifting him off the ground.

Rising higher and higher, he becomes a silhouette against the blue sky. As he catches the wind, he spreads his wings and begins to soar.

CHAPTER 15

Cole

I'm late. Too many delays and overtime meetings.

A reddish-orange sunset streaks the horizon by the time I pull into Lantern Square. The Bicentennial Festival banner still hangs from the gazebo, but workers are dismantling the art and food booths and taking down the decorations. Only a few people linger around the plaza.

With a sigh, I take out my phone to text Josie. A message from her appears:

JOSIE: Come to the pier when you get in.
COLE: On my way.

After parking near the docks, I walk to the pier. The place is bustling with a late-summer crowd. Colorful lights shine in the dusk. Familiar noises fill the air—laughter, music, and happy screams from the carnival riders.

I feel Josie before I see her. My heartbeat increases, and warmth floods my veins. She's standing by a fried-dough booth, watching the rotating Ferris wheel. She turns her head. Our gazes meet, and the smile that spreads over her face contains all the good things in the world.

I break into a run, suddenly feeling as if a year rather than a week has passed since I've seen her.

"Hi…oh!" Her eyes widen.

Hauling her into my arms, I lower my mouth to hers. *Ah, perfect.* Cherry candy, salt water, powdered sugar, Josie. My head spins. Everything inside me comes to life.

"Hi." Reluctantly, I pull away and set her back on her feet. "I missed you."

She laughs, her eyes sparkling. "I missed you too. Welcome home."

"Thanks." I brush her dark hair away from her forehead. "You said you had a bunch of stuff to tell me when I got back."

"Some of it can wait." She tucks her arm into mine. "I thought we could just hang out here, for old times' sake."

"What about new times' sake?"

"That too."

We walk toward the carnival. Pigeons flock along the weathered boards, pecking at fallen scraps of food. Two couples head into McGinty's, laughing. A chorus of shrieks rises from the Tilt-O-Whirl.

"I heard one of the new Arts Center proposals will be to restore and repaint the Ocean Carousel," Josie remarks. "They're hoping to make it a community-centered project done by volunteers. Mechanics, artists, woodworkers. A collaborative endeavor."

"I'll be happy to contribute. I have a particular fondness for that carousel. Well, for the whole pier."

"Even the Milk Bottle Toss?"

I narrow my gaze on the old game booth, where I spent many

hours collecting money, handing out baseballs, and restacking the bottles.

"Fondness, no. Gratitude, yes." I rub my hand over Josie's lower back. "If I hadn't been staffing the booth all those years ago, I might not have seen you that night. And you wouldn't have thrown yourself at me with wild abandon."

"Not that you seemed to mind," she reminds me dryly.

"Come on, man," the game operator calls. "You look like you can win a nice prize for your lady. Doesn't he, miss?"

He winks at Josie, who shrugs. "It might take him a couple of tries."

"Fighting words." Taking out my wallet, I put a few bills on the counter. "What do you want me to win you?"

"How about I win you something this time?" Josie suggests.

"You…"

She lifts her eyebrows inquiringly.

"…go right ahead." I step back to give her room at the counter.

The game operator sets down three baseballs. Josie picks up a ball, then performs a windup that allows me to admire the way her jeans stretch over her perfect dumpling ass.

She pitches, hitting two of the bottles.

The small crowd behind us cheers and applauds.

The second pitch is too far to the left. The crowd groans.

Third pitch…the last milk bottle topples.

"Nice job." Not about to miss the opportunity, I kiss her again. "Especially with the windup."

"I'll pick your prize." She studies the array of animals and toys, then points to the lower tier plastic toys that contain an unknown surprise inside. "We'll take that purple shell."

The operator hands me a plastic box shaped like a scallop shell.

"Vanessa used to have something like that when we were kids," Josie says. "It was filled with little tubes of lip gloss."

"Just what I need," I remark. "Little tubes of lip gloss."

"Maybe there's something else inside."

I open the box. Tucked against a cotton pillow is a red Lifesaver.

"Well, it's perfect for you, at least." I extend the box to her and stop.

She's gripping her hands together. Nervousness shines in her eyes.

"Jos…" My heart slams against my chest.

"Wait, wait. I have a whole speech for you." She holds up her hands and takes a deep breath. "Do you remember when I told you you were my hero? I didn't really know what that meant until now. I…" She pauses and clears her throat. "I think I fell in love with you when you saved my Halloween candy from being stolen, but I never imagined that one act would lead to the sacrifices you've made since then.

"And while I loved you twenty years ago, I love you even more now. It's taken me some time to remember how lucky I've been in life, to have had my family…to *still* have them…and then also to have you *love* me the way you do…"

Her voice breaks. Stepping forward, I tug her hard against me, gripping the plastic box in one hand. I can't speak past the tightness in my throat.

"My speech." Her words are muffled against my chest.

"Sorry." Forcing myself to loosen my grip, I release her. "Your speech."

She looks up at me, her green eyes glittering with tears. "I never want to lose you again. I don't want to dwell on the past or wonder *what if*. I want us both to focus on *what is*. What we have together."

Taking the box from me, she holds out the Lifesaver. "Cole Danforth, will you take the leap and marry me?"

"I…" I swallow hard. All these years, everything we've been through…my mind struggles to believe we're actually here. "Are you serious?"

She laughs and wipes her eyes. "I'm giving you my last cherry Lifesaver as a ring. How much more serious can I be?"

Holy....

Light explodes through me, a starfall of pure joy. I grab Josie again and plant a hard kiss on her lips that makes several people around us applaud and cheer.

"Yes." I ease back and lean my forehead against hers. Ten years ago, I'd been so happy with her, but *this*... I didn't know this kind of happiness existed.

I do now.

"Of course I'll marry you." I lift my head and settle my hands on either side of her neck. "I love you more than I ever thought was possible. I was planning to ask you too, but you're going back to California in two days."

"I know." She smiles, her face glowing. "That's part of the *bunch of stuff* we need to talk about. And I'll get you a better ring soon."

"A better ring than a Lifesaver?" I admire the shiny candy in the box. "Not possible."

As the crowd disperses, I slip the box into my pocket. Josie tucks her arm through mine and guides me away from the game booth.

"Remember that night we rode the carousel?" she asks.

"I'll never forget." I shake my head. That twenty-two-year-old boy would never have believed this bright, sweet girl would one day become his future wife.

My wife.

The calliope music on the carousel jingles. *Old times' sake.*

"Do you want to ride the whale?" I ask.

"Is that what you're calling it now?" She chuckles and squeezes my arm. "Later, yes. First, let's ride the Ferris wheel."

I lift my eyebrows. "You sure?"

"I'm sure." Biting her lower lip, she looks up at the wheel. "I have one last fear to conquer."

Pride fills me. It's not possible to love her more.

After buying two ride tickets, I return to the Ferris wheel entrance where Josie is waiting. I extend my hand. She puts her fingers in mine and tightens her grip.

"Don't let go," she says.

"I won't." I lead her to the glittering wheel spinning against the night sky. "Come on, Josie Bird. Let's fly."

EPILOGUE

Josie

One Year Later

Pushing aside the gauzy curtains, I look through the picture window at the cove. Sunlight splashes over the water where lobster boats are chugging back after a day at sea. The park and pier bustle with a lively summer crowd.

A tall man with sun-streaked brown hair steps away from the workers on the dock and starts up the path toward Watercolor Cottage. My heart gives a happy little leap as I walk to the door.

Stepping onto the porch, I shade my eyes as my husband approaches. His jeans and T-shirt are streaked with dirt, and his nose is peeling from a sunburn. The sight of him lights me with joy.

Cole smiles, his eyes creasing at the corners, and extends his arms. I hurry to hug him, not caring that he smells like boat oil, salt water, and sweat.

"How did it go?" I ask.

"We're almost ready." He squeezes me against him and sets me down, his blue eyes as warm as the summer sky. "Give me a minute to shower, and I'll tell you all about it."

We return to the cottage, and he disappears into the bathroom. While we live at the Sea Avenue house year-round, we've gotten into the habit of spending most of our summer hours at the cottage, which we've transformed into an actual studio.

Vanessa helped me redecorate, and now the interior is an airy haven of blue-and-white furniture, sheer curtains, and painted wooden shelves. Our mother's artwork adorns the walls, and a large drafting table sits near the window alongside a corkboard where I pin all my ideas.

The restoration of the Ocean Carousel is well underway, with dozens of town residents volunteering their time and talent for everything from electricity work to painting and historical research. In addition to my role as director of the restoration, I'm designing a new mural for the concrete wall beside the pier and planning my winter projects for the Arts Center.

"Dave Jamison has about twenty students and researchers onboard for the research cruise." Cole comes out of the bathroom in a cloud of steam, a towel around his waist and his bare chest glistening with water droplets. "They're going to track the sharks with satellite and acoustic tags and test E-DNA technology. That will give us a lot of data about shark migration patterns. Dave is working on research about the importance of predators to ocean conservation."

"That's fantastic." His anticipation warms me to the center of my soul. "I'm so proud of you. Has the cruise been scheduled yet?"

"Yes, for next April. It'll be a month-long partnership between Invicta and three other institutions."

He lifts his arms to scrub his wet hair with another towel. The movement makes the towel around his waist slide lower, drawing my attention to the beautifully defined muscles of his abdomen.

"And we have a pile of applications to review from other scientists who've asked to use the *RV Atlantis* next year." Cole tosses the second towel aside and rests his hands on his hips, his brow furrowing. "It'll be tough to make choices. I wish we could fund them all."

"This marine research vessel of yours might be Invicta's best investment yet." I slide my arms around his waist, breathing in his clean, soapy scent. "But I am glad you're not the one running off to chase sharks for a month. Especially next April."

"I'm not leaving you for a week, much less a month." He puts his hand on my cheek, his expression softening. "Not even to chase sharks."

He bends to kiss me. The warm pressure of his lips sparks heat into my blood. I trail my fingers over his damp chest and down to the loosely knotted towel. With a quick tug, I pull the towel off him and drop it to the floor.

"Oops," I murmur against his lips.

"Uh huh." He lifts his head with a grin. "Don't we have to be at your sister's house in an hour?"

"For what?" I rub my palms over his abs.

"Dinner." He pulls his eyebrows together. "Nathan's making blueberry pie, and you know that cop can bake."

"Oh, I almost forgot about the dinner." I lean in to lick a drop of water from his neck.

A groan rumbles from him. "You *did* write it on the wall calendar."

"Mmm. In blue ink too, did you notice?" I slide my lips across his shoulder. "My designated color for our perfectly planned schedule. I also already have next year's calendar pinned up."

"Five months before the end of the year?" He settles his hands on my hips and nudges his growing erection against me. "Now you're really turning me on."

"Go check it out." Releasing him, I step back and gesture to the new Van Gogh wall calendar pinned up in the kitchen. "In fact, you'd better write the shark cruise in since I know you'll want to be there when they set sail."

Though he frowns, disgruntled at the interruption of my caresses, he goes into the kitchen. After picking up a black pen, he flips next year's calendar to the month of April.

"They're planning on leaving around the twentieth, so—" His voice breaks off. The pen drops to the floor. He stares at the little decorated square indicating April thirtieth.

An eternity seems to pass. I grip my hands together. My chest tightens.

Cole drops the calendar page and lowers his head. All the breath escapes his lungs in a hard rush. He turns, closing the distance between us in two strides, and pulls me into his arms with such ferocity that I gasp.

"Josie." He tightens his arms around me and buries his face in my hair. He's shaking. "I once thought it couldn't be possible to love you more, but I was wrong. I love you *more*. So much more."

Tears spring to my eyes. "I love you, Cole. So much more too."

"This is incredible." He eases back, his throat working with a swallow. He puts his hand on my belly in disbelief. "When did you find out?"

"This morning." With a laugh, I put my hand over his. "I could hardly wait for you to get home."

"I'm…" He smiles, his face lighting with pure happiness. "I can't believe it."

"I can." I back up, tumbling onto the bed and pulling him down on top of me. "I've learned to believe in so many things. Especially *us*."

Tenderness and love fill his eyes. I wind my arms around his shoulders. He cups my cheek and covers my mouth with his. As we indulge in a lengthy kiss, I fall blissfully into the warm spiral of lust.

"I love you, my Josie Bird." Cole presses his lips to the hollow of my throat. "But do we have time?"

"Oh, yes." I slide my hands into his hair and bring him back up to kiss me. "We have a lifetime."

ABOUT THE AUTHOR

New York Times & USA Today bestselling author Nina Lane writes hot, sexy romances about professors, bad boys, candy makers, and protective alpha males who find themselves consumed with love for one woman alone. Originally from California, Nina holds a PhD in Art History and an MA in Library and Information Studies, which means she loves both research and organization. She also enjoys traveling and thinks St. Petersburg, Russia is a city everyone should visit at least once. Although Nina would go back to college for another degree because she's that much of a bookworm and a perpetual student, she now lives the happy life of a full-time writer.

www.ninalane.com

THE SECRET THIEF

"This book is a work of art."

Escaping the disgrace of a scandal, art historian Eve Perrin runs away to the coastal town of Castille, Maine, where she encounters a mysterious lighthouse keeper who has dark secrets of his own.

THE SUGAR RUSH SERIES

Taste the sweetness of life.

From the Stone family patriarch down to the youngest bad boy, follow the lives and loves of the Sugar Rush men in Nina's sexy, compelling series.

THE SPIRAL OF BLISS SERIES

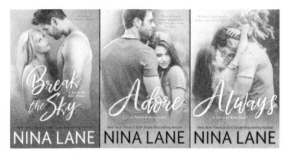

"Give me a kiss, beauty."

From an exhilarating crush to the intensities of marriage, Liv and Dean West embark on a passionate lifelong journey together. As the medieval history professor and his beloved wife face both personal challenges and painful battles, they never lose sight of the hope, humor, and devotion that belong only to them.

Liv and Dean's everlasting romance will melt your heart, turn you on, and enchant you with the power of a love to end all loves.

Printed in Great Britain
by Amazon